Promised Land

应许之地

吉狄马加 著

GUANGXI NORMAL UNIVERSITY PRESS
广西师范大学出版社
·桂林·

序一

致吉狄马加

在记忆和想象之间，摇曳着一个未知的将来，吉狄马加称之为“应许之地”。是否真的存在一块“被应许的”土地？抑或，是人在永无止境地不断创造自己的土地？

吉狄马加，我的诗歌之友：

我以创造性想象力的名义向你致敬。在阅读你这首如同预言一般烛照心灵的诗篇时，想象力在我耳畔如此低语——

记忆，就是延续人的经验言说的内容。

这世上的文化无非两类：要么是信条和宗教，要么是体验和创造。

前者的本质，是关于死亡的永恒应许；后者的本质，是关于生命的永恒应许。

前者是关乎“工具”的，后者是关乎自我的。这令人想起阿拉伯古代哲学家法拉比的话：“存在于自我的人，其自我属于自己；存在于工具的人，其自我属于他人。”

让我们用法拉比之声，用诗歌之声，齐声说：

“祝福每一个存在于自我的人，祝福属于他的各种创造性的未知!”

阿多尼斯

（薛庆国译）

Preface 1

For Jidi Majia

Between memory and the imagination, an unknown future flickers. Jidi Majia calls this "The Promised Land". Does a promised land really exist? Or are people continually creating their own lands?

Jidi Majia, my friend in poetry:

I salute you in the name of the creative imagination. In reading this poem, which illuminates the soul like reading a prophecy, imagination whispers into my ear:

Memory is the articulated content that continues human experience.

There are only two types of cultures in the world: creed and religion, or experience and creation.

The essence of the former pertains to the eternal promise of death; the essence of the latter pertains to the eternal promise of life.

The former concerns "tools", the latter concerns the self. This reminds one of the words of the ancient Arab philosopher Al-Farabi: "he who exists in himself, his self belongs to himself; he who exists in tools, his self belongs to others."

Let us use the voice of Al-Farabi and the voice of poetry to say in unison:

"Bless everyone who exists in the self, and bless the various creative unknowns that belong to them!"

Adonis

Jami Proctor Xu

（徐贞敏译）

序二

这个世界的一部分

吉狄马加的诗学在人类的起源中寻求它的灵感气息。这就是为什么我们不能把它与对人类状况和环境的反思割裂开来。从信仰引领他相信“应许之地”那一刻到现在，环境的危险使我们再次寻找这个神话般的地方。我们现在发现，这个地方必须由人类来保存，而不是交付给某个神的手中，每次它都离我们的未来更远。因此，诗歌是我们必须遵循的道路的一个指标，它受到诗歌和部落的大师们的启发，他们给了我们必须从那里出发的智慧。在这首诗中，吸引人的是吉狄马加在大自然中找到了通往这块“未来土地”的道路，如果我们学会如何建设它，它仍然可以存在。这就是为什么像《应许之地》这样的诗歌是一种必要的向导，可以使我们继续“成为这个世界的一部分”。

努诺·朱迪斯

（姚风译）

Preface 2

Be Part Of This World

Jidi Majia's poetics seek its inspiring breath in the origins of humanity. That is why we cannot dissociate it from a reflection on the condition and circumstances of man from the moment when belief led him to believe in a "promised land" to the present, in which environmental dangers lead us to seek, again, this mythical place which, we now discover, must be preserved by man and not delivered into the hands of some god, each time further from our future. Therefore, poetry is an indicator of the way we must follow, and it is inspired by the masters, both of poetry and tribe, who gave us the wisdom from which we must depart. What attracts in this poetry is the way Jidi Majia finds, in nature, the way to this "future land" that still can exist if we learn how to build it. And that is why poems such as "The promised land" are a necessary guide so that we continue to "be part of this world".

Nuno Júdice

序三

“众生的仪式”

1

我在今夜暗红的血月之下写这篇文章，似乎很应景。今夜的月亮，被大地投下的斜影所笼罩，勉力发出微弱的光芒，像内地小镇的门廊灯，又像大山某一村落中的一盏孤零零的路灯；举目遥望孤悬天外这颗温润的球体，仿佛自己置身在另一个时代，几乎是忘形于另一个星系，一个未来的世界，抑或一个过去的时间，一个天地间正缓缓铺排的巫术仪式，令人印象深刻。今晚，我们每个人都会短暂地沉浸在一个降生那一刻就已经知道的承诺中：有一种美好不可方物，有一种圣洁震慑肉身。一个新的时代，一个深陷不安的当下，在这漆黑的11月的天空中，飘浮着一颗暗红的月亮，星星像湖上的茶灯一样飘来飘去，过往人类所有的妄行，人世间所有失去的美好珍贵，借用古先贤的话来说，所有的民族，所有的生命都曾经被理解过，一切都被原谅了。

不出两个小时，夜空又恢复了平时；在埃及，世界领导人再次开会，研讨如何应对过往他们那些聊胜于对我们所居住的气候灾难的应对；在美国，人们充满愤懑走向投票站（中期选举）；饥荒、战争、洪水、油船泄漏，造成大规模的海面浮油、石油价格暴涨暴跌，新冠病毒继续肆虐。然而，今夜月食仿佛给予人类一丝怜悯和希望，涤荡了一次黑暗的天空，在未来的时间里，一个发生巨大变化的世界，天体现象似乎预示着（几乎要实现），“人还是 / 这个世界的一部分”。正如吉狄马加在《应许之地》这首伟大的诗歌宣言的结尾所预言的那样。

世居中国西南大凉山的彝族或诺苏人的服饰多为黄、红和黑三色。恰好我的家乡澳大利亚土著人民的服饰也流行这三种色调。今夜月食——月亮也忽而黄色，忽而红色转黑：田野一片昏黑，就像太阳或燃烧的余波；火红维护健康，温暖人民（澳大利亚许多地方的土壤呈红色）；太阳的黄色。就像吉狄马加所有的诗歌，这首长诗《应许之地》，虽然暗喻所有的土地，所有的生命，实际歌咏的却是他的祖籍，故乡——大凉山，他要书写“生命的节日”，那些几千年来，有助于维持人与人之间、人与所有其他生物之间以及与河流、山脉和气候之间的尊严关系的文化、传统和习俗。

这首诗的核心意象就是火塘，族人围着火塘，谈论和传递“怎样去迎接生，还要如何去面对死”的传统智慧。而“唯有火光”——在这个时空弯曲、预言、时而讽刺、时而怀旧的神谕中，变身为“千年智慧的集散地”——“唯有火光能让围坐在四周的人 / 真切地看见那些黑暗中的东西”。在他的诗中也是如此，火塘的功能类似欧美的壁炉，我们贴近壁炉，也是在聚集和反思；

今晚也是如此，间红间黄的月亮，为我们寻常人生中遗忘之物投下智慧之光，并且聚光我们生活的数字盲区。

所以你看，我写下我对吉狄马加这首类似金斯堡的《嚎》一般激越的文字，是一桩应景之举。月食中今晚的月亮一时间是血色的，就像黑色土地上的火塘，星星像不眠之夜的孩子，零散孤悬天际。做如此观，这首长诗让人想起此前吉狄马加的诗作。

> 给我们血液，给我们土地
> 你比人类古老的历史还要漫长
> 给我们启示，给我们慰藉
> 让子孙在冥冥中，看到祖先的模样……
>
> ——《彝人谈火》

2

一首诗可以同时唱出多少个音域，仍然还是一首诗？如果说一个深沉而独特的声音——毕摩（彝族祭司）祈祷，作法，幽远，缥缈，同时直指当下，切入现实；如果一首诗在地，深置于传统，栉风沐雨几百年；如果一首诗是一条河流，渐次汇聚无数小溪成为滚滚巨流；如果一首诗弥漫穿行在女人的舞步中，那舞步“踏着大地隐秘的节拍”；如果一首诗背后隐现，被顽强的价值观加持（反复回旋在这首长诗的和弦中）——那么一首如此宏大而富于宣言的诗，富于远见，富含预言，必定会受到这个山地民族的珍怀并被长久吟诵。

委实如此。《应许之地》读起来就像吉狄马加描述的那条“黑色河流”；山地逶迤出殡送灵的队伍，诗人眼中蜿蜒流过家乡山谷的那些“黑色河流”一样，这首诗纪念过去，敬畏从未过去的，庆祝（即使他们也在哀悼）代际传承的传统，仪式发生地，模式，古老的歌曲和传唱方式，个人的尊严（生与死），以及族群对每个人的生活的影响。

我了解葬礼，
我了解大山里彝人古老的葬礼。
知道古时诺苏人在大山上的葬礼。
（在一条黑色的河流上，
人性的眼睛闪着黄金的光。）

我看见人的河流，正从山谷中悄悄穿过。
…………
沉沉地穿过这冷暖的人间。
沉沉地穿过这神奇的世界。

——《黑色河流》

诗人吉狄马加描绘的《应许之地》似一股上升气流，代表“不可救药的复数”（引用路易·麦克尼斯的话）。吉狄马加曾在他的诗《致自己》中这样说：“但是这一点可以肯定 / 如果没有大凉山

和我的民族 / 就不会有我这个诗人。”或许《应许之地》，描写一个因河流而生的族群，一个珍爱诗人的族群。这首诗读起来也像是一份群山的宣言。

3

阅读《应许之地》，是在阅读一种预言，预示我们的地球和我们人类深度陷入“全新世”样态，将当下的恶托邦时代推向一个在功能、语言和地区多样性、沉浸感方面更少更弱的加强版的恶托邦时代。古老的智慧，更商业化，更抽象，更科学，更同质化，更少人道，更少野性，更虚假，更虚拟，这个“全新世”的物种比及当今更稀缺。回望那逐渐逝去的世界，窥测即将呈现的未来——任性的现在所貌似应许的那即将到来的土地——诗人回顾过去，现在迷失了（“他羊群的踪影早已消失于昨天”），或者勉强还在坚持，当古老的智慧，因其深置于乡土，代代相传，教会族人如何生，如何死，热爱乡土，保持尊严，珍惜幸福。

通过回溯历史，展望未来，这首诗帮助我们驻停发展的脚步，透过诗人所见所思，思考一下，我们即将失去些东西。虽然有些怀旧，但诗人很清楚：“那不是回家的路；过去的小路 / 已隐没于漂泊者的颅底。”诗人似乎想要说的是：全新的现实，亟待我们找到全新的看待和命名的方式，逝去的就让它们逝去，我们必须放下，继续前行（伯特兰·罗素也有类似的说法）。一如既往，诗人希望我们看到，在此关头，诗歌既承受了最大的威胁，又是人类最为需要的——如果《应许之地》对人类还有任何意义的话，因为诗歌是当今最具人性化和生态化的看待事物和存在的方式，诗歌的使命就是尊重和呵护地球上所有生命的神秘性、多样性和多元性。极而言之，最受威胁的恰恰是我们最需要的，诗歌精通“人们为什么继续生活”的通关密码。如果我们还有理由继续生活在即将到来的世界中，在步入《应许之地》之前，就应该警醒我们的后代觉醒过来，对万事万物抱持“惊讶”有多么重要——即对事物的神秘、野性——每每讶异惊喜的本能，而对于这种觉醒，舞者和诗人就能派上用场，因为这个世界一直需要诗人——巫师——去看到没有被注意到的细节，说出原本无法表达的东西。

吉狄马加在这首新作中，表达了对未来的谨慎的希望：“他们的诗人也许还存活于世。”他接着说：“我完全相信 / 虽然他还站在固定的位列歌唱，/ 但他手中熊熊的火把却照亮了世界。”

4

“让古老的语言在最新的法律上。”在《应许之地》中，诗人呼唤道，“变成这个世界的文本”。在这里，吉狄马加似乎在呼应珀西·雪莱的名言：“诗人是世界无冕的立法者。”虽然，他说的“最新的法律”将会以多种语言出现，每一种语言都是特定地方和人民的习语。如果诗歌要赢得民心，那么未来仍将是“不同方言的词语构成的群山、峡谷和森林”。“词语中有机的斜坡。”他继续说，并注意到这首诗经常重复的一个音符：有机的东西，从智慧的人类与峡谷、河流、火和神秘世界的互动中产生的东西，自身天然具有美德、语言和思想。有鉴于此，这首诗也赞扬了语言的多样性、思想和方法的差异性。

《应许之地》特别希望彰显完整性、真实性和特殊性。在社群中，在真实的地方，个体的人类生活和心灵得到教育。这一切，曾经是大多数人的寻常故事，“他们还要回到原野，寻找万物新婚的毡子”，这一切都与“工具理性的实用主义”相悖，与抽象和千篇一律背道而驰。理所当然，诗歌奋起捍卫、保存和示范所有这一切。

诗人兼预言家希冀的乐土（与他厌弃的恶托邦相反），这首诗论证说，是一种改良版的现代性。常规的现代性带来种种恶习，如数字化、思想的抽象、贫乏的自我概念（“星星……/……与我们的灵魂却若即若离”；“对不同的悲伤做出相同的描述”），肤浅和做作（诗末提到的硅乳房植入物），丑陋和狭隘的一致性（“……如同克隆的产品”；“从每一扇窗户看到的都是同一种景象”）——不一而足。不妨说，这些恶习并非不可救药——透过传统、诗歌、原住民的教训、“大地的气息”、真实的天气，和活生生的灵魂，透过野性的生活经验，丰富、多样性和人性化的语言——均可获得矫正。从而，《应许之地》将被赎回，如果能够回忆起从前，并经过诗人、先知和长老的提醒（如果有可能找到代替毕摩的地方），人们将摆脱无助和无奈——现今他们的生活局限在物理意义上的存在、顺从和购买，每个个体，甚至是“微小的昆虫”，都将参与“生命准备的仪式”，所有的灵魂都会重塑，并随着时间的推移而延续下去。

5

诗人在这首诗中清楚地表明，前进的路并不是简单回到过去（“不是回到过去”）；前行，如果你愿意的话，意味着深入：“那只是个体生命 / 对逝去的精神的追念。”在当今的世界上，吉狄马加仍然抱有希望，哪怕他的故乡乃至世界各地，扑面而来全是负面的现象，现代的自我仍然会知道如何在生活中对“传统”保持敬畏（沉默）。就我而言，这是一个令人信服的、神谕的思想，在诗的开头就已经出现：“这是自我献给传统的沉默。”欲要求得文明的生存，写意的生活，如果你愿意的话，诗歌，古老的传统，定时轮替的风习可以助你一臂之力，而要抱持这种沉默，心必须觉醒，思必须谦卑，不妨说像林中的动物一样思，感，知，欲。如此，拯救我们的是一种被铭记的崇敬——可以说，在我们许多语言中都一一实践过（“不属于任何一种语言”）——走向世代相传的智慧，走向未被文字记述过的智慧。这种智慧体现在地球的万事万物之中，隐含在人类形形色色的文化传统、行为方式之中。这种智慧承接我们祖先的种种教诲，既不符合现今的商业利益，也不支持特定的党派路线。“这是自我献给传统的沉默。”

6

公元2世纪和8世纪之间，一位名字被遗忘的诗人在巴勒斯坦写了一首诗。在我看来，这首诗没有过时，依旧抒发灵魂深处的希冀——这才是世间最可珍贵的——心的渴望，渴望蹚过“时间之河”：

不畏前路漫漫，艰难险阻，
驾战车，左冲右突，
人世间徘徊，凝视辉煌，
戴上冠冕，荣耀加身，
为美好歌唱，写下诗篇，
赞美上苍、天界和人间，
要知道活着的意义
并目睹死人的异象。
蹚过火河，了解闪电。

我们在这片可怕、光荣和传奇的地球上做如此短暂的驻留。近乎白驹过隙。一个世纪，依地质纪年的尺度，不过草木一秋。我们活在当下，被赋予了一颗渴望的心，一副能够运动、爱和睡眠的肉体，我们还富有各种感官，能感知，有痛感，我们还能思想，有记忆，当然，还传承需要学习和继承的传统，以及先祖的种种承诺，这种种承诺，或被实现，或遭到背弃。我们身负匡正乱世的使命：过度的商业化，窒息了精神与心灵；我们步履极为艰难，一路上还会有骗子引诱我们，还会有专制限制我们的自由，抑制我们的声音，误导我们爱谁，爱什么，何处摆放我们的激情，安排我们的生活。当然，尽管我们历经种种磨难和坎坷，尽管我们的理想希冀屡屡落空，仍有其他人会爱我们。直到大限来临，每一个个体，都会从地球上逝去。

内心深处，我们意识到人生就是一场美丽的悲剧，阳光普照大地，雨露滋润万物，人生欢乐和痛苦相互交织，并走向不可避免的结局。整个世界，大地母亲，我们永恒的家园，芸芸众生，一直在继续，并且将在没有我们的情况下继续存在。我们怀着炽热的心，生来就渴望、奋斗、希望、喜悦和悲伤，我们知道我们的日子和所有重要的日子某一时刻就会戛然而止。

换句话说，生而为人，就是要知道人生苦短，所有的生命，尤其是我们自己的生命，都会走到尽头。我们如何生活得好，并在既有的知识中保持清醒，这就是我们人类的许多麻烦所在。佛教帮助其修行者觉悟如何对抗无常之河，离苦得乐。然而，这种有关诸法皆空的高妙智慧，得道入门者少之又少。

我们活着的时候，有所希冀，有所憎恶：比如肉体痛苦、物质贫困、失政、流行病、不义。我们的希冀清单上包括青春、美丽、夏天、真爱、名声、健康、假期、生活本身。这份清单上还包括创造性——人类狂欢节的压轴节目，而创造力最易磨蚀，乃至腐坏，如果我们对此忽略，未能及时给予足够的关心和关注，也肇始人性的种种弱点在作祟：当然，我的意思是人类伟大的美德——我们所有人可能会以不同的方式命名——我们知道文明不发生畸变，社会不至脱轨，我们绝对需要这些美德（同情，公正的法律，精神和信仰的自由，对美的热爱，分寸感，尊严），才能促成人类彼此之间，以及与其他造物和谐相处的可持续生活方式，真正重视生态健康，维持目前的温和的气候总体不至失序，从而危及人类及文明的持续存在。

我想说，诗歌比任何其他社会实践都更好地见证了佛教意义上的诸法无常，并公正地对待我们的有涯人生。只要人类还在继续发声，歌唱，这就是诗歌之所以为诗歌的题中应有之义。有些人，比如格雷格·奥尔，相信抒情诗的演变是为了让我们在困境的创伤中保持清醒。当然，在我们所知道的每一种文化中，诗歌均没有缺席。由于诗歌与人类共始源，在已知的所有语言、地点和时代，诗歌都见证了在如此短暂的美丽和恐惧的世界中活着和有意识的感觉具有什么意义。诗歌永恒，而我们作为个体，必有一死。

设若有人问及诗歌如何帮助我们渡过存在的危机，我会这样回答他：诗歌关乎人生苦短的永恒苦恼，诗歌以特别方式，给出了有益人生的答案。

（1）诗歌见证了我们希望留给未来的快乐，这些快乐透过诗歌比我们的个体生命更恒久。

（2）诗歌寻到了合适的音韵形式，跨越时空的韵律和文字的结合，把我们混乱无序的情感加以有序巧妙的编排（悲伤、嫉妒、愤怒、欲望、缺乏），从而予我们的苦难以慰藉；换句话说，诗歌驯服难以忍受的苦痛，使之变得可以忍受——诗歌此时蜕变为神奇的火塘或壁炉，我们与他人一起围坐，暖意融融。

（3）诗歌呈现世界和我们内心的美德——否则我们会轻视或忽视，并拒绝让善良、可爱和荣誉这些美德不能得以彰显，诗歌也倾向于保存吉狄马加在这首诗中所说的“传统”——在我们的生活中，在我们赖以生存的土地上，继续葆有维护诸如美丽、正义和尊严这些美德的必要条件。

在所有这些方面，诗歌对现实进行抒情修复，复苏易于凋谢之物，并诱哄我们参与保护世界。虽然《应许之地》被装扮成一个老年吟游诗人的悲观预言，吉狄马加这部新作恰恰在示范如何对现实进行抒情修复。吉狄马加深知，正如他所有的诗歌所做的那样，诗歌旨在保存重要的东西，持久的东西。诗歌驳斥虚假和卑鄙的事物，是对苦短的人生以及当下这个缺憾多多的人世间诗意的矫正。

7

窃以为，这就是吉狄马加在这首诗中所号召的——创造美好的生活（不仅仅是为我们自己），帮助所有人在《应许之地》理想地过活：

· 以优雅和庄重的姿态参加死者的节日。

· 知道如何、何时、何处在众生的仪式中占据自己应有的位置。

· 熟悉曲调，懂得如何吟唱某些传世隽永的歌曲，因为这些歌曲唱出了人世间所有生与死的秘密。

由于诗歌恰恰就是这些隽永恒久歌曲的文辞部分（忘记了它，我们就忘记了自己）；通过吟咏歌唱，人们才会跳起生命的舞蹈（生命的本义就是且歌且舞）。

8

也就是说：因了诗歌，诀别人世之前，我们意识到我们参与并延续的事业不会结束，而这种伟大的生活（在我们永恒的具体时刻生活了一段时间）就是诗歌所要延续的东西，诗歌时时提醒我们的生。正如吉狄马加所言，诗歌这种人类传统，生命仪式，才是货真价实的乐土，只要我们都能尽心尽力维护诗歌，人类将永葆这一桃花源生生不息。诗歌承载人类，诉说着我们深刻的人性——我们每个人都是独一无二的，分享更广博的人性——直到我们的肉体生命终结之日。诗歌向我们讲述过去的生活，栩栩如生的人们，好似你我一样的今人，诗歌也会向我们的后人继续讲述你我今人的生活。诗歌是一个容器，像一个罐子或一艘船，容纳着一种精神、一种寂静、一个空间；诗歌赋予声音以形状，诗歌会呼吸，就像我们的身体内置的机能在发挥作用。即使我们停止呼吸，诗歌仍旧持续存在。

但是，如果诗歌要永续存在，如果我们的生活要持续显示某种意涵，那么读者就必须阅读诗歌，并在生活中回忆起他们对过去和未来以及他们自己和现在的诗歌责任——记忆、见证、保存方式和地点、价值观、习俗和传说的抒情责任——以及所有培育涵养伟大的诗歌传统的那些诗歌前辈，至少是吉狄马加在《应许之地》中所歌咏的那些了不起的人——该诗的叙述者、诗人本人、毕摩、舞者。他们手持火炬，踏着有节奏的舞步，唱着鼓舞人心的歌谣。换言之，诗歌所承载的传说，必须不断地被言说、被观察、被尊重、被表演，否则诗歌的生命就会终结，一旦生命终结，《应许之地》必然沦为平庸无奇的反乌托邦，吉狄马加在本诗中一再警示这一点。

9

据说，托钵僧鲁米写出一首诗，就会在上面跳舞。鲁米透过舞步的旋转，被带入一种诗意的狂喜状态。我从未目睹吉狄马加仿习鲁米，在自己的诗歌之上舞姿翩翩，但我确实亲耳听过他的歌声，一个言辞得体、举步有致的人，陶醉在自己的歌声中，而欣喜若狂。他的这首长诗是他多年温良性情的见证，和虔诚沉浸于诺苏萨满教义的结晶，在我看来，与其说《应许之地》是一篇布道词，不如说是诗人神志处于狂喜状态所产生的真实表达。来到这首诗的后半部分，诗人一口气铺排了十四行之多他心中的桃花源应该呈现的样貌，看似随意，其实节奏铿锵，这些理想的实例可以说是对美好人类生活中所有重要事物的隐喻；诗歌何以为必须吟咏歌唱的理由，而这些理由，我们因为深陷当下的数字生活中，惨遭无视，但由于诗人的不懈吟唱，我们终有一日，回到

《应许之地》，铭记不忘：

群山，赤脚，铠甲，苦荞，
石磨，金色的皮碗，月琴，马布，
宝刀，鹰爪杯，锅庄石，
英雄结，蜜蜡，送魂经，白色的毡子，
山风，谱碟，谚语，史诗，
护身符，习惯法，超度，火焰，枪，
父子连名，酒，表妹，血亲，婚配，神鹰，
智者，马鞍，服饰，
传统，火把节，勇士，火葬地，
自由的迁徙，尊严，死者，
可以赴死的，崇尚黑色的，内心的，热情的，
万物有灵的，盟誓的，亲近骨血的，
身份，认同，庄重，格局，英勇。

“他们知道人活下去的理由”是编制这样一份幸福生活清单的主旨。我们可以这样解读：清单试图反驳眼下的过度商业化实践、人工制品和相关的价值观已经异化为当下人生的意义（我们为什么乃至我们如何继续生活）。理所当然，这份《应许之地》的要件带有浓厚的吉狄马加故土所属的诺苏文化的色彩。但读者几可肯定——作者透过这首诗示范了他对于文化及语言多样性的必要性的一以贯之的主张和坚守，以及多年来，他身体力行促进中国诗

歌与世界诗歌跨语际对话所做的一切，因此，上述漫漶滔滔十四行之多，未来人类桃花源必备的标记，就表征人类任何一种特定语言或生活中的所有此类事物。透过这首诗，诗人再一次申明在伟大的存在盛会上，为生者和死者代言，恰恰是诗歌与生俱来的使命——除非我们希望无常获胜。因为，正如他所说：“人的占卜是神在左右，/ 而神的预言往往只能让人来确证。”

10

一首诗就是一个语言事件。之所以如此，是因为词语代表了生命中每一刻可能发生的事件，如果我们都还记得我们应该如何理想地过活。吉狄马加的《应许之地》恰恰就是一桩这样的事件。尽管该诗字里行间浸透了一种绝望的情绪，但这种绝望源于一种爱之深责之切的动机——对我们所有人、对生命、对野性和高雅文化的永不熄灭的爱，尤其是对诗歌及其使命的爱。这首诗，一如诗人的历来的写作基调，沉静中不乏希望。我们周遭毕竟弥漫着太多非诗意的事物，人类一直受困数不胜数层出不穷的难题和危机，危及生存，威胁到他一直试图歌唱的“存在仪式”，他的希望谨慎有节制，完全情有可原。情势毕竟如此糟糕。尽管如此，诗人仍以希望的基调，结束了这首以《应许之地》为名的长诗。诗歌虽然是脆弱的容器，但依然可以承载人类穿越黑暗走向光明的信心，而人类面临的困境，则应归因于我们无视既有流传至今的传统。因为事实是：诗歌和歌唱几乎就是人类曾经拥有的一切，对于《应许之地》，这两点几乎总是丰盈自足的。

马克·特雷尼克

（傅浩译）

Preface 3

The Ceremony of All Being: Jidi Majia's "Promised Land"

1.

It seems fitting that I write these words under a blood moon.

The moon tonight, cloaked in the slanted shadow thrown by the earth, puts out a low glow, like a porch-lamp burning in an outback town, or like a solitary streetlamp in a high mountain village; and looking up at this tender, distempered orb, one feels one is alive in another era, almost in another galaxy, a future world or a past time, which is still remembered tonight in this slow and shamanic ceremony of the cosmos. Tonight, you inhabit briefly a promise you know you were born into: of beauty beyond measure, of holiness incarnate, incarnadine. A new time, a deeply troubled and unsteady present moment, is spoken inthis tenebrous sepia moon afloat in a black November sky, and stars bob about like tea-lights on a lake, and all that you have not done right, all that will never again be intact in the world, is suffered to be said in the old words all peoples, all beings once understood, and all is for a moment forgiven.

And after an hour or two, the night goes back to being November in ordinary time; in Egypt world leaders meet again to consider their inevitably compromised and piecemeal responses to the climate catastrophe that we inhabit; in the US the people go angrily to the polls; there are famines and wars and floods and oil slicks and oil shocks and renewed outbreaks of pandemic. And yet, the eclipse leaves a trace of mercy and hope like a wash across the dark skies that in the future time, a vastly changed world,which the celestial phenomenon seemed to foretell (almost to enact), "people are still part of this world," as Jidi Majia's speaker puts it at the end of this great manifesto of a poem.

The colours of Jidi Majia's people, the Yi, or Nuosu, ofthe high mountains of Liangshan, are yellow and red and black. These are the colours, as it happens, of the Indigenous peoples of my home continent, Australia. And those are the colours of the star country tonight: the black of the field, like an aftermath of sun or burning; the red of the fire that keeps the country well and warms its people (the red, also, of the soil in so many parts of my land); the yellow of the sun. Like all of Jidi Majia's poetry, this long poem, "Promised Land," though it speaks of all lands and contemplates all lives everywhere, rises where he himself arose—the mountain landscapes of his people, "the festival of life" among them, the cultural practices that have helped sustain dignified relations among people and between people and all other beings and with the rivers and mountains and the climate, for many thousands of years.

In Jidi Majia's poem one central image is the hearth, the firepit, the villagers gathered in a circle around a fire, talking and passing on traditional wisdom about "how to greet life and face death." And "only the firelight"—transfigured by Jidi Majia in this time-bending, prophetic, and sometimes ironic, sometimes nostalgic oracle into "the distribution center of the wisdom of a millennium"—"can let those gathered ... clearly see the things in the darkness."And so it is in his poem, itself a hearth around which it feels we are called to gather and reflect; and soit is tonight, the red and yellow moon throwing a wise light on things normally lost on us in the everyday and overlit digital blindness of our lives.

So you see how apt it is that—under pressure from my friend Hunter, who is editing this book and who has to translate these words against a tight publishing deadline—I write these words about Jidi Majia's elegant "Howl" of a poem, under a moon tonight that is made of blood and resembles a fire pit in the black lands, the stars scattered about like sleepless children? His poem seen in this light brings to mind some words from a much earlier poem of Jidi Majia's.

Give us blood, give us land
You are more ancient than history
Enlighten us, console us
Let children in darkness see their ancestor's appearances...

2.

How many registers can a poem sing at once and still be a poem? If a deep and distinctive voice, the voice of the Bimo (Yi priest), say, holds it true in its coursing back and forth and far and deep; if topography grounds it and the weather of centuries plays through it; if it is a river many smaller rivers join; if the dance steps of women "treading out the secret rhythms of the earth" trip through it; and if values (struck often like the notes of a chord this great poem is strung on)sustain it—then a poem this big and declamatory, this visionary and discursive, can hold together like wild mountainous country long cared for.

And so this poem does. "Promised Land" reads like the "black river" Jidi Majia describes in his poem of the same name; this grand new poem is like a procession for the dead that, like those "black rivers" the poet has seen pass through his home valleys, honour what has passed, respect what never passes, and celebrate, even as they mourn, human traditions carried forward, the patterns of place, the old songs and ways, the dignity of each person (in life and in death), and the power of community (as the poet turns it in this new poem) to each individual life.

I know ancient Nuosu funerals on the great mountain.
(On a black river human eyes flicker with golden light.)
I've seen a river of people quietly passing through the valley.
I've seen a river of people overflowing with ripples of sorrow.
Passing heavily through this changing world.
Passing heavily through this mystical world.

"Promised Land" is an upwelling, as "incorrigibly plural" (to quote Louis MacNeice) as the land the poet Jidi Majia knows he speaks for. In his poem "For Myself", Jidi Majia once himself said this. "But this I can be sure of:/ If there were no Greater Liangshan and my People didn't exist/ then I, the poet, wouldn't exist." Perhaps "Promised Land," a great country of rivers, is where all that country was carrying this poet. For it reads like a manifesto of mountains.

3.

"Promised Land" is a kind of prophecy, commenting on the state of the earth and of us humans upon it deep in the "Holocene" by throwing forward to a dystopian time a little less functional, less linguistically and regionally diverse, less steeped in old wisdom, more mercantile, more abstracted, more scientistic, more homogenised, less humane, less wild, more false, more virtual, more denuded of species even than our own. And from that diminished near future—that coming land, which the wayward present seems

吉狄马加画像　岳敏君 绘

to promise—the poet looks back to older times, now lost ("his flock of sheep vanished long ago"), or barely hanging on, when older wisdom, schooled by connection to country, held and schooled humans in life and death and community and dignity and beauty.

By throwing forward and back in this way, the poem helps us stand a step back from where we are, as the poet sees it, and think about what we are about to lose before we lose it. Although the poem is nostalgic, the poet is clear: "these aren't the roads home; the small paths of the past/ have disappeared." What the prophetic speaker of this poem seems to want is this: that we find new ways of saying and seeing things, and each other, the way they actually are, not the way they may once have been and are no long, nor the way we are told they are or ought to be (Jidi Majia makes telling reference in the poem to Bertrand Russell's famous words to this effect). And poetry, as ever, the poet wants us to see, is what is what is most under threat and also most of what is required if the promised land is to hold much promise at all—a deeply humane and ecological way of seeing and being in the world, in which the mysterious and diverse and plural nature of all life on earth is revered and conserved. What is most at risk is also what we most need is language that "know[s] why people keep living". If there remains reason to keep living in the coming world, our descendants in the land the present promises will need to know how to wake to their own "astonishment," to the mystery and wildness of things, and for that awakening, they will need the dancers and the poets, for the world has always needed the poet—the shaman—to see what goes unremarked, to say what is otherwise unsayable.

And Jidi Majia in this new poem expresses the cautious hope that in the future "their poet might still be alive." He goes on: "I fully believe/ even though he still stands in a fixed position and sings, / the torch in his hand will illumine the world."

4.

"Let ancient languages in the newest laws," one Bardic passage of "Promised Land" declares, "become the texts of the world." Here Jidi Majia seems almost to echo Percy Shelley's famous utterance: "Poets are the unacknowledged legislators of the world." But for JidiMajia, the "newest laws" will be spoken in many languages, each an idiom particular to and as specifically wise as its places and peoples. If poetry prevails in the ways of women and men, the future will still be hirsute with "forests composed of words from different dialects". "Words have a natural slope," he goes on, striking a note the poem often repeats: what is organic, what grows from intelligent human interaction with the world of canyon and river and fire and mystery, has virtue, and so it is with language and thought. Diversity, plurality, of language and difference of thought and approach are, for this reason, praised, too, in the poem.

What is wanted in the promised land is integrity, authenticity, particularity. Individuated human lives lived and minds schooled in communities, in real places. All this, once the remit of most of humankind, "who would return to the wilderness to search for the wedding rug of all living things," is set against "the pragmatism of instrumental rationality", against abstraction and sameness. And all this, of course, poetry defends and conserves and models.

The promised land the prophetic speaker hopes for (as opposed to the dystopia he imagines) seems, on the evidence of the poem, to be a modified species of modernity, its bad habits—toward digitization, abstraction of thought, meagre conceptions of self ("the stars seem both close and far from our souls"; "identical descriptions of different sorrows"), shallowness and artificiality (the silicon breast implants alluded to late in the poem), ugliness and narrow conformity ("clusters of ... concrete buildings are like cloned goods"; "the same scene is seen from every window")—its bad habits all tempered by tradition, by poetry, by the lessons of Indigenous peoples, by recollection of the "breath of the earth" and the scent of the actual weather and the soul of some actual facts, by lived experience of the wildness of things, by a wealth and diversity and humanity of language. The promised land the poem hopes forwill be redeemed, it seems from the helplessness of its present dispensation, if its people can recall, at the bidding of the poets and prophets and elders (if any may be found to take the Bimo's place), that, more than just existing and conforming and buying, each being, even "tiny insects", takes part in a "ceremony of life", that all souls constitute and perpetuate through time.

5.

The way forward, the speaker of this poem makes clear, is not the way back ("this is not returning to the past"); the way forward, if you like, is the way deeper in: "it is individual lives/ remembering a spirit that has perished." In the world Jidi Majia still holds out hope for, against the weight of evidence around him in his homeland China and around the world, modern selves will still know how to keep open a silence in their lives to "tradition". This, to me, is a compelling, oracular thought, that appears almost as an aside early in the poem: "This is the silence the self offers to tradition." What is necessary to the survival of civilization, to livable life on earth, is, if you like, the nothing that only poetry, that ancient tradition, fashions, the silence that only the awakened heart, the humble mind, the animal soul, is capable of; what will save us is a little remembered reverence—practised, as it were, in every one of our many languages ("it doesn't belong to any one language")—toward wisdom passed on hand to hand for generations, toward wisdom implicit in the earth and evident in cultural practices and modes of behaviour and address that have not forgotten what our ancestors knew, and which do not conform to any party line of commercial verity.

"This is the silence the self offers to tradition."

6.

Somewhere between the second and the eighth centuries, a poet, whose name is forgotten, wrote a poem in Palestine. And it seems to me this poem still speaks today for what it is a human heart—real estate no one can ever own (though many will try)—yearns for, what a body hopes for, while it has its chance to swim a while in "the river of time":

To rise on high / and descend below,
to ride the chariot's wheels / and explore in the world,
to wander on earth / and contemplate splendor,
to draw on the crown / and sound Glory,
to utter praises / and link letters,
to utter names / and behold what is
above and below, / to know the meaning
of the living / and see the vision
of the dead. / To ford rivers of fire / and know lightning.

We are so briefly here in this terrible and glorious and storied earth. We are so soon gone. Even a hundred years passes like a season of geology. And while we are here, we are given these hearts in their longing and these bodies in their moving and loving and sleeping and these senses in their apprehension and hurt and these minds which remember and these traditions to be learned and carried on and these promises to be broken or fulfilled, this work to be done; and while we are here with all this "all too much for us", to be getting on with, there will be some of our kind whowill try to scam us and curtail our freedom and still our voices and tell us whom to love and what to do with our lives and where to put our passions; and there will be others will love us notwithstanding all our faults and all that did not want us to flourish in our. And then, each of usa species of one, will go extinct.

Deep down we live a beautiful tragedy that unfolds in sunlight and in rain, in joy and suffering, toward its inevitable end. And all the while the world, our mother, our eternal home, the rest of who we are, goes on, and will long go on without us. We, with our burning hearts, are born to yearn and struggle and hope and delight and grieve, alive in the knowledge that our days and all that mattered in them will end.

To be human, in other words, is to live with the knowledge that all living, including in particular our own, comes to an end. How we live well and stay sane in that knowledge is what a lot of our human trouble is about. Buddhism has helped its practitioners understand that how we fight against the river of impermanence is how we suffer. Be carried by the river, Buddhism suggests, but few find that easy.

While we live, some things we wish would pass, refuse to: our pain, our poverty, bad governments, pandemics, injustices. Other things we wish would stay pass: youth, beauty, summer, true love, fame, good health, holidays, life itself. And finally, some things we need to hold if the human carnival, the festival of creation, is to carry on, and they seem always at risk of corroding or corrupting, through human neglect, through lack of care and attention, through the actions of the lesser angels of our human natures: I mean, of course, the great virtues, which all of us might name differently, but which we know we need if chaos is not to ensue (compassion, just laws, freedom of spirit and belief, love of beauty, a sense of proportion, a quality of dignity), and I mean sustainable ways of living with each other and with the rest of creation, ecologically responsible practices that do not endanger the temperate climate that more or less allows all human life and civilization to happen at all.

Poetry, I want to say, and better than any other practice, bears witness to these three species of impermanence and does justice to our impermanent lives. It has fulfilled that role as long as humans have known how to speak and sing. Some, like Greg Orr, believe that lyric poetry evolved for the purpose of keeping us sane in the trauma of our predicament. Certainly, in every culture we know, there is poetry. Certainly, it is the original and the essential literature, and certainly in all languages and places and times it bears witness to what it feels like and what it means to be alive and conscious for such a short time in a world of beauty and dread that will go on without us.

In case anyone should ever ask you how poetry helps anyone through an existential crisis, let this be said about poetry: it is, in these specific ways, the answer to which impermanence is the question.

(1) It bears witness to the joys we wish would stay, and keeps them said longer than our lives can.

(2) It consoles us in our pain by finding pattern and fellowship across the ages in it, and byordering otherwise chaotic and inchoate feelings (grief, jealousy, sorrow, anger, desire, wanting); it shapes often unbearable feelings, in other words, into habitable forms—into hearths to sit with others round.

(3) By embodying the virtuous habits of the world and of our hearts, which we otherwise disdain or neglect, and by refusing to let goodness and loveliness and kindness and honourgo unspoken, poetry has tended also to conserve what Jidi Majia calls in this poem "tradition"—the necessary conditions for the perpetuation of beauty and justice and dignity in our lives and in the lands we are sustained by.

In all these ways, poetry runs lyric repairs on reality, conserving what always otherwise atrophies, and cajoling us to participate in the preservation of the world. And although it is dressed up as the gloomy prognostication of an ageing bard, it is just this work that Jidi Majia's "Promised Land" performs. For poetry, he knows, as all his poetry affirms, is for the conservation of what counts, what lasts; it is the refutation ofwhat is false and meagre, of all that inevitably falls short in the ways of men and women lived in the everyday and hasty world.

7.

And here, I think, is what, specifically, the speaker of Jidi Majia's poemenjoins us to do—to fashion a good life (not only for ourselves), to help all of us prosper in the promised land:

- To join with grace and gravitas the festivals of the dead.
- To know how and when and where to take one's proper place in the ceremony of all living.
- To know the tune and to sing the words to some true songs in which all life and death are sung.

For poetry is the words to the old songs (forgetting which, we forget ourselves); it is the steps to the dance that goes on (and in which life itself is carried on).

8.

Which is to say: When we end, something we participated in and perpetuated does not end, and this great living (lived for a while in our embodied moment of eternity) is what poetry sustains and what it reminds us while we live that we are living. This human tradition, this ceremony of life, as Jidi Majia puts it, is our true promised land, and it never ends as long as enough of us attend to its conservation. Poetry carries us on, speaking our deep humanity—that unique piece each of us is, and the wider humanity in which we share—when we are no longer here to say and enact it. Poetry speaks past lives to us, the living, as if they were our own, and it speaks our living on to others who come after. Poetry is a vessel, like a pot or a boat, that houses a spirit, a silence, a space;itgives shape to voice and form to breath, the way our bodies do in life. And poetry lasts when we do not.

But if it is to last, if what we lived and what our lives meant are to go on signifying anything, societies must read poetry and live with some recollection of their poetic responsibilities to the past and the future as well as themselves and the present—lyric responsibilities of memory, of witness, of the conservation of ways and places and values and customs and lore that counts—and some among those who cultivate the great human tradition, must be at least a few of what Jidi Majia calls in this great poem, variously, the narrators, the poets, the Bimos, the dancers. Holding the torch, stepping out the dance, singing the songs that sustain what sustains us. The lore that poetry carries, in other words, must continue to be said and observed, respected and performed, or it will cease, and the promised land will become the bland dystopia JidiMajia's poem prophesies.

9.

Rumi, it is said, danced up his poems. The Dervish dance, the spinning, transported that great poet to the ecstatic state from which his poems arose. I have not seen Jidi Majia dance, but I have heard him sing, and I have seen him in an ecstasy of delight at words well spoken and steps well performed. And his long poem, the culmination of many years of tender witness and devoted shamanic utterance, feels to me much less like a sermon than the truthful articulation that the intoxication of the spirit gives rise to. Deep into the poem are fourteen free-verse lines that list, randomly but rhythmically, instances that might be said to stand as metaphors for all that counts in a good human life; instances of what it is that poetry must sing so that we, who otherwise, in our digital lives, forget to value, will not forget to love in our promised land:

Mountains, bare feet, armor, buckwheat,
grindstones, golden leather bowls, moon lutes, mabu,
jeweled knives, eagle claw goblets, stone pillars upholding the pot,
hero's knots, honey wax, the mantra for sending off souls, white felt,
mountain wind, genealogy, proverbs, epics,
amulets, common law, releasing souls from purgatory, flames, guns,
father and son's linked names, liquor, female cousins,
   blood relatives, marriage, sacred eagles,
sages, saddles, apparel,
traditions, the Torch Festival, warriors, cremation grounds,
free migration, dignity, the dead,
those who can meet death, revere black, heartfelt, passionate,
animistic, taking oaths, intimate with flesh and blood,
identity, recognition, solemnity, structure, valiance.

"They know why people keep living" is how this list concludes. Which might be read to mean: these practices and artefacts and values are what living means and why and how we carry on. As is only right, this litanyrises specifically from theNuosu culture to which JidiMajia belongs. But you can be sure—from all he says in this poem about the necessity of diversity of view and language, and from all he has done in China over many years to promote multilingual conversations in poetry, that this sonnet of a list of true good things stands for all such things in any one of our particular languages or lives. And JidiMajia, in this poem, wants as to know that speaking for the living and the dead in the great pageant of being is poetry's work—unless we want impermanence to win. For, as he puts it, "people's divinity is controlled by the deities, / and the deities' prophecies can usually only be confirmed by people."

10.

A poem is an event in words. It is an event in words that stands proxy for the kind of event each moment in life might be if we remembered to live it properly. Jidi Majia's "Promised Land" is such an event in words. And although it purports to despair for us, in truth it arises from his unquenchable love for all of us, for life, for wildness and high culture, and above all for poetry and the purposes it serves. This is a poem, like so many Jidi Majia has written, of quiet hopefulness. If his hope is tempered by all that is not poetic and all that diminishes us and all that threatens the very ceremony of being he has always sought to sing, we can forgive him. For much is not well in the world. Still, he ends with hope a poem that begins with "the promised land." Poetry and song might seem brittle vessels to carry humanity across the rising tides and through the intemperate weather our neglect of tradition has conjured, but poetry and song are all we ever had, and they have nearly always been enough.

Mark Tredinnick

吉狄马加画像　岳敏君 绘

吉狄马加画像　岳敏君 绘

目　录

应许之地

你看，那里是应许之地！
当然不是上帝许诺给犹太人的礼物，
那里没有流淌着白色的牛奶。
这或许就是一块未来之地，
并非另一个乌托邦，而是现代性
在传统的笛子与球体之间
构筑的玻璃和模制品的世界。
那里星星与头的距离没有改变，
但它与我们的灵魂却若即若离，
噢！时间，你改变并终结了
我们通往永恒之路的第七种方式。

那时唯一的鹰还盘旋在高处。
因为它的存在，生命的意义
才被赋予了某种可疑的证据。
从最高的地方俯瞰大地，哦，星球！
倾斜的梯子承载着穹顶的意志，
那是心知功能的棋盘，纵横交错的
高速公路闪着油亮灰色的光。
那不是回家的路，过去的小路
已隐没于漂泊者的颅底，再没有
吹竖笛的儿童在山冈上挥手，
他羊群的踪影早已消失于昨天。
峡谷的倒影投向断裂的天空。
河流被切成数字的香肠。世界的同一性。
让七月发怒的暴雨以反复无常的
恸哭，向两岸喘息的面孔咆哮。

向这些物种致歉，要等一个世纪还是千年？

那儿是梯级电站的博物馆，

千差万别的设计被人称道。
河流裸露的石头对天空报以无声的叹息。
噢，太阳！佩戴酋长的面具
聆听白色狐狸的嘶吼。人是万物的尺度，
数量可观的猴子没有表决权，
自言自语的真理只能被后世证明。
不是回到过去，那只是个体生命
对逝去的精神的追念。
这是自我献给传统的沉默，
不属于任何一种语言。
任何语言的不足只有一种，
那就是对不同的悲伤做出相同的描述。
成群立体的水泥建筑物如同克隆的产品，
这是现代星球的漂浮物，
不是似曾相识，而是同一张脸。

这是想象中的未来之地：

他们千百次地离开过这里，但他们

还会回去，那是因为祖灵还在那里，
说不清这是一种责任还是义务。
再不用凭着记忆去推开古老的木门，
那仅仅是存活于梦里的一道影子。
这是一座智能的城市，山寨的名字对
后代而言已经非常陌生，如果讲述者
想告诉他们，已并非那么容易。
这里标准的街区经过科学的规划，
就连每天的基本食物也大同小异。
这不是卡夫卡的城堡，但对人的性质一样。
建筑材料像一块块透明的晶体，
没有泥土和四季的呼吸留下的味道。
他们的生活被网络完全地支配，
不需要真相，穿越任何一个障碍物
都能在穹顶目睹到闪烁的电子眼。
不用再骑着马在峡谷边行进，
名马达里阿宗[1]只存活于词典，

[1] 达里阿宗，彝族历史上一匹名马的名字。

不会听见圆形赛马场欢呼的声音，
那时这种山地马肯定还没有灭绝，
只是除了作为动物园孩子们的宠物，
当然它还会是一种值得保护的物种，
谁知道它曾获得过多少赞颂与光荣，
无数勇士因为它的奉献而名垂青史。
三色马鞍的制作者，失去了存在的价值，
纵然他的精品被存放于都市的博物馆，
参观的游人留下赞赏的目光，这不是
一个属于马的时代，骑手的光环暗淡，
寻找马蹄铁的预言已经没有意义，
从远处山脊风能旋转叶片送来的问候，
告诉刚刚醒来的人类，时代已发生了巨变。
那时的导航比今天要快，新的交通工具
能将诸位送到任何一个你想去的地方。
这是科学的胜利，这是技术的胜利，
但这绝不是人的全部的胜利，因为我们
失去了最后一个能完整吟唱摇篮曲的人。

噢！应许之地，在时间铸造的玻璃那边，
不是夏日的雨季，在那无法确定的反面，
泪花与雨水结成了不可分离的轴线，
它让粗糙的山脉变得如同情侣的睡姿。
一支高腔的民谣被反复乘方荡气回肠，
那些远离传统的游子，为时下的生存
已遗忘了词根所积蓄的全部意义。
房间里没有火塘的位置，微暗的火
只呈现于年老者渐渐风化的记忆。
那样的情景会在偶然间被唤醒，
黝黑的皱纹里注满浑浊的泪水。
哦，火焰！一千年智慧的集散地
曾被你照亮，从父亲传授给儿子，
怎样去迎接生，还要如何去面对死，
让母语鲜活的词飘浮于永恒的空白，
唯有火光能让围坐在四周的人
真切地看见那些黑暗中的东西。
然而在这数字化的居住区域，
能提供的并不是差异的需求，

抽象的人将完全主导这个世界。
在钢铁和水泥搭建的混合物中
那是新的材料塑造的未来的家园，
如果还有讲述者活着，他的眼睛
将面对滚滚而来的太阳
像他们的祖先一样向万物致敬。
他的声音在此刻是唯一的存在，
音质的骨骼支撑着光亮的天际，
因为他的召唤，河流会被感动
群山的肃穆超过了任何一个时刻，
每一个生命，就是那微小的昆虫
也会集合起自己的队伍，
赶去参加一个只为生命准备的仪式。
今天的召唤者并不是毕摩[1]
那完全是他的召唤，从这网格编织的城堡
找到了一条路，尽管这条路并不通往
我们消失的那个传统的世界，

[1] 毕摩，彝族传统社会的祭司。

但他却让我们看见了久违的穿斗结构的天宇
以及神话中巨人的木勺。

这是电气和升降机搭载的庙宇，
从每一扇窗户看到的都是同一种景象，
老人的目光投向赭红色的地平线，
陷入沉思，是想去听布谷在春天的鸣叫，
要解开遁入时间的褶皱，唯有密钥的口弦
能告诉你自己命运的多舛和人生的无常。
孩子从电脑上收看偷猎者在北极
肢解海豚的过程，而书桌上的白纸
已被杀戮者意念的指纹倾泻染红。
为了供养这群人类家园的留守者，
他们的儿子或者父母已经在这个国家的
四面八方，为了一份工作竭尽了全力。
只有岁末他们才能回到这个被称为
祖居之地的故乡，哦，谢天谢地，
他们除带回了积攒的金钱就是异乡的方言，
在戏谑之后母语的问候哽咽于喉咙。

没有他们不想坐的列车，货币的轨道
能让求生者旅行于任何一个地方。
这是立体的街区，规范的准则已
成为模式，高耸的电缆连着透明的山脉。
机器的嗡嗡声从远处传来，
集体就业的人群在玻璃幕墙的那边，
他们的影子有序而如同固定的装置。
噢，这个星球上的德高望重者，
尽管你们操作不同的语言，穿着不同的服装，
你们的心灵是否能在同一个时刻
进入一个完全被道义和真理照亮的隧道？
谁能相信你们会做出一个准确的判断，
在现实未经加工的两个弧形之间，
为什么不让局部凹陷于整体的肚脐，
把求同存异的想法告诉更多的人，
那些微弱的东西，是一粒石子、一枚纽扣、一张
信纸，当有人在耳边呢喃，反复地、持续地、善意地，
那幸运的斗篷就会从天而降
童年丢失的木碗将神奇地出现在眼前。

那些古老的瓦板房已不存在，
它是群山的孩子，白色袅袅的炊烟
让天空和大地充满了爬行的梯子。
在山脉盆腔和腹部睡眠的磁性的族人
是太阳燧石的影子唤醒了他们。
鹰仍然在宁静的虚空瞩望移动的印记，
一只蚂蚁翻动土壤发出敏感的声音。
逻辑的马铃薯的王国，在饥饿的年代
苦荞原子的构造救活过一个种族的婴儿。
玉米的来源，在诗歌和传说里发出烘烤的香味，
半农半牧的生活，谚语不可更改的根据，
当智慧的传诵敲击奥秘之门
还是火焰用辩词的方式告诉了大家
那些隐藏于语言中的非理性的巨砾。
不可计算的红色的辣椒，啊诺苏[1]的家园！
你以刺人眼目的银幕方式，在每一个外墙上

[1] 诺苏，凉山彝族聚居区自称为诺苏，意思即黑色的民族。

挂满了秋天旺季红色迭起的组画。
啊不同方言的词语构成的群山、峡谷和森林，
在这里找到陌生人要比找到亲戚困难！
肩上搭着披毡在山路上唱着
情歌的穿小裤脚的月琴手！
被雌野鸡的叫声召唤到山梁羽毛闪闪发光的雄鸡！
剪羊毛节堆放在敞坝上比雪还要白的羊毛！
啊每一个男孩童年养的金色的大公鸡！
火把节的选美，对美的传统的评价
在光与影的流淌中心灵与外貌得到了统一！
啊千百年来跟随史诗迁徙的黑色的种羊！
我们咬碎了一口吞入喉头和胃部的格言！
在这片土地上现实与影子吞噬了荒诞
成为镜子里复数狂欢的生活。
每一个火光照亮老人和孩子的夜晚，
少女的羞涩、掩着嘴的窃笑、含着梦境的眼睛，
啊在口弦和月琴之间的鸟翼，准备飞翔！
接纳新的生命，火焰的影子第一次
在婴儿的眸子留下对光的惊奇。

噢，迎接死亡，为了最后撞击荒诞的盛宴，
他们宰杀牲畜不是一场游戏
而是在完成一次死亡与生命的告别，
没有任何仪式能放置于它之上，他们的哀号
让别的动物与致命的石头一起落下。
无法见证死者重生的卵石与锤的语言
只有在这里，也只能在这里
才能体会到群体对一个人的价值。
不知道是惩罚还是救赎，现代的人类
在水银般的琉璃长廊里呼吸升降，
乳房的膨胀不是奶水而是糟糕的硅胶，
而繁衍生命的任务给了白色的试管。
让至亲者回去，像婴儿一样踢动天体的摇篮，
不仅仅是为了倾诉才选择母语，这其中
群山的主体才是我们精神直达的颅骨。
噢，这也许不是我们想象的那个时代，
能背诵英雄谱系的孩子越来越少，
在送葬队伍中能领唱的人
已变成稀有动物！

地球上最大的荞饼，给饥饿的弱者以及
需要帮助的人一点空间，
让古老的语言在最新的法律上
变成这个世界的文本！
词语中有机的斜坡，赞颂你
以烧红的石块祛除污秽！
让钻牛皮的人喜出望外！
发出嗞嗞声音燃烧的松明，父亲的化身！
肋骨两侧的群山，大地左倾的陡坡，
火塘赫梯拉巴[1]的山脉：黑色的鞍子
被银饰预约的宴席。
诺苏的子孙，如果你们还没有忘记
在库史[2]的时候为祖灵送上萨拉博[3]酒壶，
而祭拜者的手中将打开盐和酒的内脏！
面对永恒的太阳，呼唤，抛撒细碎的金银！

---

[1] 赫梯拉巴，彝族传说中的大力士，是他摔死了天王派来强征赋税的格惹阿比，并点燃火把烧死了害虫，后世为纪念这个日子而演变了火把节。

[2] 库史，彝语彝历新年的意思，时间在每年阳历的 12 月 20 日左右。

[3] 萨拉博，一种彝族古老的酒壶。

两个世界的钱币，
在生与死的分界处，黑和白交媾的影子
嘶喊缠绵着
唯有神枝的鸟儿把银杯留给了自己！
不是绝对的进步也不是
现代意义上的落后！
噢，你们给了足够多的水
而又拿走了仅有的一点盐。
如果没有了灵魂玛瑙上那红色的穗须
再积极的盘子又有何用？

无数阳光缠绕的混凝土的阶梯，
这里听不见黑山羊咩咩叫的呼唤，
噢，在那远方，从高处往下跳的羊群
扬起的尘土遮住了谁的眼睛？
黑山羊是祭祀祖先必不可少的牺牲，
那是一个智能的时代，人的心灵
注定还会踟蹰于无尽的生与死的峡谷，
他们还要回到原野，寻找万物新婚的毡子。

要从陡峭的低处爬到最高的地方，
摔跤、格斗、骑马，那些古老的竞技，
或许只有返回到金黄体格的器官中，
人类的儿子才能高扬雄性和创造的旗帜。
这是应许之地，它隐匿于宇宙的另一个纬度，
它并非现实的存在，对应于时间之河的
未知的没有名字的抽象的疆域。
群山，赤脚，铠甲，苦荞，
石磨，金色的皮碗，月琴，马布[1]，
宝刀，鹰爪杯，锅庄石，
英雄结，蜜蜡，送魂经，白色的毡子，
山风，谱碟[2]，谚语，史诗，
护身符，习惯法，超度，火焰，枪，
父子连名，酒，表妹，血亲，婚配，神鹰，
智者，马鞍，服饰，
传统，火把节，勇士，火葬地，
自由的迁徙，尊严，死者，

---

[1] 马布，彝族一种古老的吹奏乐器。
[2] 谱碟，彝族家支的谱系，男人都能背诵。

可以赴死的，崇尚黑色的，内心的，热情的，
万物有灵的，盟誓的，亲近骨血的，
身份，认同，庄重，格局，英勇。
他们知道人活下去的理由，
就是让大家摆脱虚无给彗星加上的尾巴，
这不是科学的迷信，人的占卜是神在左右，
而神的预言往往只能让人来确证。
这是应许之地，人类的种族还要有一段时间
才能进入它透明如同白昼的高速车站。
那些居住者，是这个族群未来的子孙，
他们别无选择，那是因为他们只能从
自身的觉醒中获得惊愕、野蛮和愤怒的力量。
噢，应许之地，就是到了那个时候
他们的诗人也许还存活于世，我完全相信
虽然他还站在固定的位列歌唱，
但他手中熊熊的火把却照亮了世界。

如果说我们已经看到了那个未来，
它在时间的驿站像一对孪生的兄弟，

一个朝着天堂，另一个面对黑暗，
而世界在那一刻变得很小
北极的冰水滴满了你的额头，撒哈拉沙漠
的月光在一只手提箱里怀孕。
而那一天正好是迎送祖灵的时间。
不是活着的人才围坐在那里，当木碗里的
酒送给嘴唇，同时滋长痛苦和快乐的闪电，
为人性中的善加冕吧，让恶出生时
就开始死去，让善成为今天之后唯一的道德，
给未来留一些可怜的东西，不要用锄头
去加害它们，千姿百态的物种
在田园之外它们已生存了千百万年。
它们遭遇的痛苦和境遇，不是今天才出现过
只是这个世纪远远超过了从前，而不幸的是
动物最先遗忘的就是同类遭受的厄运。
让时间在四维中真的成为可能，让善的种子
再次回到人的子宫，让罗素说给未来人的话
被天上的星星和父亲般永恒的太阳证明是对的。
让不同的母语在算术里获得新生，是因思维方式不同，

而并非工具理性的实用主义。
只有当人类的种族在火把的引领下再次返回旷野，
每个人的脸上都漾溢着古铜色的油彩，
朵洛荷[1]的舞步踏着大地隐秘的节拍，牛头上的红布
宣告了自然力与人的原始欲念重逢于战栗的蜂巢。
回到大地的婚床吧！让人的生殖力成为重量的一部分，
这是生命的节日，当然也是人的节日。

噢，应许之地，但愿到那时候人还是
这个世界的一部分。

2022年1月10日至17日

[1] 朵洛荷，彝族古老的一种女性集体跳的舞蹈。

吉狄马加画像　朱成林 绘

吉狄马加画像　科奇什·安德拉什·山多尔 绘

Promised Land

Look, there is the promised land.
Of course it is not the gift the Lord promised to the Jews;
there is no white milk flowing there.
It might be a future land,
not necessarily another utopia,
but a world of glass and molded goods
constructed by modernity
among traditional flutes and spheres.
There, the distance between the stars and our heads hasn't changed,
but the stars seem both close and far from our souls.
O, Time, you changed and terminated
the seventh way on our path to eternity.
Back then, the sole eagle was still hovering high.
Its existence meant the meaning of life
was given dubious proof.
Looking down on the earth from the highest point, o, Planet.
The tilted ladder bears the weight of the dome's determination.
It is the chessboard of the mind's capabilities; the crisscrossed
highways glow glossy gray.

These aren't the roads home; the small paths of the past
have disappeared in the base of the wanderer's skull, never again will
there be
a child playing a recorder on the hills, waving his hands.
His flock of sheep vanished long ago.
The canyon's reflections are cast into a fractured sky.
Rivers have been sliced into digital sausages. The uniformity of the
world.
The erratic mournful cries of furious July rainstorms
roar at the faces gasping for air on both banks of the river.

Do we wait a century or a millennium to apologize to these species?

There, it's a cascade power station museum;
the multitude of different designs are praised.
The exposed river stones
return silent sighs to the sky.
O, Sun, donning the chief's mask,
listening to cries of the white fox. Humans are the measure of all
creation.
A considerable number of monkeys don't have the right to vote.
Truths spoken by the self can only be proven by later generations.
This is not returning to the past, it is individual lives
remembering a spirit that has perished.
This is the silence the self offers to tradition,
it doesn't belong to any one language.
There's only one type of deficiency in any language:
offering identical descriptions of different sorrows.
Clusters of three-dimensional concrete buildings are like cloned goods,

they are debris of the modern planet;
not deja vu; rather, the same face.

This is the imagined future place:

They have left this place thousands of times, but they
will return, because the ancestral spirits are still here.
It is unclear if this is a responsibility or a duty.
They no longer have to rely on memory to open the ancient wood gate;
it is only a shadow surviving in dreams.
This is a smart city.
The names of the mountain villages
are completely unknown by later generations. If the narrator
wants to tell them, it won't necessarily be easy.
The standardized city blocks here have been scientifically planned;
even the basic daily foods are virtually the same.
This is not Kafka's castle, but for humans, its nature is the same.
The building materials are like pieces of translucent crystal;
there is no scent left from the breath of the earth and the four seasons.
Their lives are completely dominated by the internet.
There's no need for actual facts; no matter what obstacle they pass
through,
they can see the flickering electronic eyes on the dome.
There's no more need to ride horses around the canyon.
The famous horse, Dali Azong, [1] only survives in dictionaries;
it won't hear the cheers around the circular racetrack.
In those days, these mountain horses weren't yet extinct;

[1] Dali Azong is the name of a famous horse in Yi history.

in addition to being pets for children in zoos,
they were a species worthy of protection.
Who knows how much praise and honor they received;
countless warriors made a name in history due to their horses' dedication.
The maker of the tri-colored saddle has lost the value of his existence,
even though his products are stored in city museums,
and tourists look at them with admiration; this is not
an era belonging to horses, the halo of horse riders has gone dim,
the prophecy of finding the horseshoe is meaningless;
the greetings sent from windmill blades on distant mountains
tell a recently awoken humanity this age has changed dramatically.
Back then navigation was faster than it is today, new means of transportation
can take everyone any place they want to go.
This is a victory for science, and a victory for technology,
but it is in no way a complete victory for humankind, since we have
lost the last person who could sing an entire lullaby.

O, promised land where the glass is cast by time,
it is not the summer rainy season; on the indeterminable opposite side,
tears and rain have formed an inseparable central axis,
transforming rough mountain ranges into the sleeping positions of lovers,
a powerful high-pitched folk song moves us repeatedly;
those who've strayed from tradition to survive in the present
have forgotten all the meaning accumulated in word-roots.
There isn't a place for a fire pit in the room; dim fire
only appears in the slowly eroding memories of elders.

Occasionally those memories are aroused,
filling dark wrinkles with muddy tears.
O, Flames. The distribution center of the wisdom of a millennium
was illuminated by you, passed from father to son,
how to greet life and face death,
making the vivid words of the mother tongue float on eternal blankness.
Only the firelight can let those gathered around the circle
clearly see the things in the darkness.
Yet, in this region of digitalized dwellings,
it isn't different needs that can be provided;
abstract people will completely dominate the world.
In composites built of steel and concrete,
it is the future homeland molded by new materials.
If there is still a narrator living, his eyes
will face the sun rolling this way
and pay tribute to all living things as his ancestors did.
Now his voice is the only presence,
the skeleton of timbre supports the luminous horizon.
His summoning will move the rivers;
the solemnity of mountains transcends any moment.
Each life, even tiny insects,
will assemble their ranks
and rush to take part in a ceremony for life.
The summoner of today is not a bimo.[1]
It was his summons that found a path
from this woven mesh castle,
even though the path did not lead

[1] Bimos are traditional Yi priests.

to our vanishing traditional world,
but he let us see the Chuandou [1] structure skies that have long disappeared,
and the mythical wooden spoon belonging to the giant.

This is a temple where people are transported by electricity and lifts,
the same scene is seen from every window.
The elder's gaze is cast toward the burnt sienna horizon,
sinking into deep contemplation, since he wants to hear the cuckoos' spring chirping.
To unravel the wrinkles escaping into time, only the secret key of the mouth harp
can tell you the vicissitudes of your fate and the impermanence of life.
A child watches the process of poachers in the North Pole on the computer
dismembering a dolphin, and the white paper on the desk
has been dyed red by the fingerprints of the killers' minds pouring down.
In order to support those who remain in humanity's homeland,
their sons or parents have already worked tirelessly all over the country.
They can only return to this so-called ancestral homeland
at the end of the year, o, thank goodness.
Aside from the money they've accumulated, they can only
bring back the dialect of another place.
After jokes are made, the mother tongue gets caught in the throat.

---

[1] Chuandou is one of the two primary framing systems in traditional Chinese architecture. The Chuandou system uses pillars and transverse tie-beams.

There aren't any trains they don't want to ride,
currency tracks allow survivors to travel anywhere.
This is a three-dimensional city block, fixed standards
have already become the model, towering electric cables link transparent
mountains.
The hum of machines can be heard from the distance,
the collective employment crowd is on the other side of the glass curtain
wall,
their shadows are orderly like fixed units.
O, virtuous people of this planet,
though you work in different languages and wear different clothes,
can your hearts in the same moment
enter a tunnel completely illuminated by justice and truth?
Who can believe you'll make an accurate judgment?
Between two raw arcs of reality,
why not let the parts be sunken in the whole navel,
tell more people the notion of seeking common ground.
Those weak things are a pebble, a button, a piece of paper,
when someone whispers in your ear repeatedly, continuously, kindly,
the lucky cloak will fall from the sky,
the wooden bowl lost in childhood will magically appear.

The ancient plank-roofed houses no longer exist,
they were the children of the mountains; white chimney smoke spiraling
up
filled the earth and sky with crawling ladders.
It was the shadow of the sun's flint that awoke
the magnetic clansmen sleeping in the pelvis and abdomen of the
mountains.

The eagle is still in the tranquil void looking for traces of movement,
the ant rummages the soil making a sensitive sound.
The potato kingdom of logic in an age of famine,
the structure of bitter buckwheat atoms saved a People's infants.
The origin of corn scents roasted in poems and legends;
the half-farmer, half-herder life, the unalterable foundation of proverbs,
when widely shared wisdom knocks on the door of mystery,
it is the flames that plead with people
to tell them about the irrational boulders hidden in language.
Incalculable red peppers, O, Nuosu [1] homeland.
You use dazzling screens to fill every facade
with continuous red paintings in the peak of autumn.
Ah, mountains, valleys, and forests composed of words from different dialects,
it is harder to find a stranger here than it is to find a relative.
The moon lute player wearing peg leg pants
singing on the mountain road, wearing a felt cape.
The rooster with glistening feathers called to the mountain ridge by the female pheasant.
The fleece whiter than snow piled in the village square during the shearing festival.
Ah, the golden rooster every boy raised during childhood.
The beauty pageant during the Torch Festival, traditional beauty standards,
the heart and external appearance become one in the flow of light and shadow.
Ah, black sheep that have followed the migrations in the epics for thousands of years.

---

[1] The Yi who inhabit Liangshan call themselves Nuosu, meaning the Black People.

We have chewed apart the maxims we gulped into our throats and stomachs.
On this land, reality and reflections have swallowed the absurd and become
lives of complex carnivals in the mirror.
Every night the firelight illuminates the elders and children,
the young woman's shyness; she titters with her mouth covered,
her eyes filled with dreams;
ah, the wings of birds between the mouth harp and the moon lute are about
  to soar!
Receiving the new life, for the first time flame shadows
leave wonderment at light in the pupils of the infant.
O, welcoming death to finally strike at the feast of absurdity.
Their slaughtering of livestock is not a game,
it is to complete a farewell to death and life,
no other ceremony can be placed above it,
their wails make other animals fall with the fatal stones.
The language of pebbles and hammers that cannot witness the resurrection of
  the dead,
here, and only here,
can it experience the value of community to an individual.
I don't know if it's punishment or redemption, modern humanity's
breath rises and falls in mercury-like glazed corridors,
breasts swell not from milk, but from horrible silicon,
and the role of reproducing life is given to white test tubes.
Let loved ones return and kick the cradle of the celestial body like infants,
not only choosing the mother tongue to pour out their mind; among these
are the main part of the mountains, the skull our mind goes through.
O, perhaps this isn't the age we imagined,
fewer and fewer children can recite the genealogy of the heroes,
Those who can lead the singing in funeral processions have become rare

animals.
The biggest buckwheat cakes in the world provide the weak who are hungry
and those who need help a little bit of breathing room.
Let ancient languages in the newest laws
become the texts of the world.
Words have a natural slope, blessing you
with red-hot stones to dispel filth.
Let those who drill the cowhides be overjoyed.
The hissing pine torches in flames, my father's reincarnation.
Mountains on either side of the ribs, leftward leaning steep slopes of the earth,
fire pit of Hetilaba[1]: the black saddle
is a banquet reserved by silver adornments.
Nuosu descendants, if you have not forgotten,
give the ancestral spirits a salabo[2] wine jug during Kushi[3],
and the hands of those offering sacrifices will open the entrails of salt and liquor!
Facing the eternal sun, call out, and sprinkle fragments of gold and silver!
The coins of the two worlds tangled
at the dividing line between life and death, the shadows of black and white copulating
cry out lingering feelings.
Only the bird of the divine branch keeps the silver cup for itself.

---

[1] Hetilaba is a strongman in the Nuosu legends. He pushed to death Ge're Abi, the man sent by the emperor to impose taxes, and he lit a torch to kill the harmful insects. Later generations developed the Torch Festival to commemorate this day.

[2] Salabo is an ancient Yi wine jug.

[3] Kushi is New Year in the Yi language. The Yi New Year is around December 20 on the Gregorian calendar.

This is not absolute progress and it is not
backwardness in the modern sense.
O, you've given enough water
but taken away the little bit of salt there was.
Without the red tassels on the soul agate,
what use are positive plates?

Countless concrete steps wrapped in sunlight,
here one can't hear the bleating of the black goats,
O, in the distance, whose eyes are covered by rising dust
when herds of goats jump from heights?
Black goats are indispensable sacrifices for ancestral worship.
It was an age of intelligence, people's souls
were destined to linger in the endless canyons of life and death,
and they would return to the wilderness to search for the wedding rug of all living things.
To climb from the lowest parts of the cliff to the highest places,
falling, wrestling, horseback riding, those ancient competitions,
perhaps only returning to the organs in the golden body can
the sons of humanity raise the flags of masculinity and creativity.
This is the promised land, hidden in another dimension of the universe;
it doesn't actually exist, it corresponds with the unknown,
abstract, nameless territory of the river of time.
Mountains, bare feet, armor, buckwheat,
grindstones, golden leather bowls, moon lutes, mabu,[1]
jeweled knives, eagle claw goblets, stone pillars upholding the pot,
hero's knots, honey wax, the mantra for sending off souls, white felt,

[1] The *mabu* is an ancient Yi wind instrument.

mountain wind, genealogy[1], proverbs, epics,
amulets, common law, releasing souls from purgatory, flames, guns,
father and son's linked names, liquor, female cousins,
blood relatives, marriage, sacred eagles,
sages, saddles, apparel,
traditions, the Torch Festival, warriors, cremation grounds,
free migration, dignity, the dead,
those who can meet death, revere black, heartfelt, passionate,
animistic, taking oaths, intimate with flesh and blood,
identity, recognition, solemnity, structure, valiance.
They know why people keep living:
to break away from the tail nothingness adds to the comet,
this isn't scientific superstition, people's divinity is controlled by the deities,
and the deities' prophecies can usually only be confirmed by people.
This is the promised land, the human race needs a period of time
before it can enter its high speed station transparent as day.
Those inhabitants are the future descendants of this race;
they have no other choice, because they can only gain
the power of astonishment, savagery, and anger from their own awakening.
O, promised land, at that time
their poet might still be alive; I fully believe
even though he still stands in a fixed position and sings,
the torch in his hand will illuminate the world.

If we say we've already seen the future,
it's like twin brothers at the station of time,

---

[1] Geneaology here refers to the Yi clan family tree. All Yi males can recite it.

one facing heaven, the other facing darkness,
and the world becomes very small in that moment,
arctic ice water drips all over your forehead, Sahara
moonlight becomes pregnant in a suitcase.
And that day happens to be the time to welcome and send off ancestral
spirits.
Those who aren't living are sitting around there; when the liquor
in the wood bowl is given to the lips, lightning
that simultaneously brings pain and pleasure,
crown the good in human nature, let evil begin to die
when it is born, let goodness be the only virtue from today onward,
leave some pitiful things for the future, don't use a hoe
to harm them, thousands of species
have existed for millions of years beyond the fields.
The pain and situations they've experienced didn't only appear today,
it's just that this century has far surpassed the past, and unfortunately
the first thing animals forget is the misfortune of their own kind.
Let time become truly possible in four dimensions, let the seeds of goodness
return once more to people's wombs, let what Russell said to those in the
future
be proven right by the stars and the eternal fatherly sun.
Let different mother tongues gain new life in arithmetic, because of different
ways of thinking rather than the pragmatism of instrumental rationality.
Only when the human race is led back to the wilderness by torches
and every face is covered in bronze oil paints
will the Duoluohe [1] dance steps tread on the secret rhythms of the earth,
and the red cloth on the bull's head proclaim that the power of nature
and human's original desire have once again reunited in the trembling

[1] Duoluohe is an ancient Yi women's group dance.

beehive.
Return to the marriage bed of the earth! Make people's fertility part of the weight,
this is the festival of life, and of course it's also the festival of the people.

O, promised land, I hope at that time
people are still part of this world.

Jami Proctor Xu
（徐贞敏译）

Terre Promise

Regardez, voici la terre promise.
Il ne s'agit pas, bien sûr, du cadeau que le Seigneur a promis aux Juifs;
aucun fleuve de lait blanc n'y coule.
Ce pourrait être une terre future,
pas forcément une autre utopie,
mais un monde tout de verre et de produits moulés,
fruit de la modernité,
entre les flûtes et les sphères traditionnelles.
La distance entre les étoiles et nos têtes n'y a pas changé,
mais les étoiles semblent à la fois proches et lointaines de nos âmes.
Ô Temps qui passe, tu n'es plus le même et tu as mis fin
à la septième voie que nous foulons en chemin vers l'éternité.
À l'époque, l'aigle seul planait encore dans les hauteurs.
Son existence signifiait le sens de la vie,
confirmé par des preuves d'origine douteuse.
Toisant la terre du plus haut point, ô Planète.
L'échelle en diagonale porte le poids de la détermination du dôme.
C'est l'échiquier des capacités de l'esprit; les autoroutes
qui le sillonnent brillent d'un gris reluisant.
Ce ne sont pas les chemins du retour; les sentiers d'autrefois

ont disparu à la base du crâne du vagabond, et il n'y aura plus jamais
d'enfant jouant de la flûte à bec sur les collines en remuant les mains.
Son troupeau de moutons a depuis longtemps disparu
et le canyon se reflète sur un ciel fracturé.
Les rivières ont été découpées en saucisses numériques. Uniformité du
[monde.
Les cris lugubres, erratiques, des orages furieux de juillet
rugissent aux visages à bout de souffle présents sur les deux rives du fleuve.

Devons-nous attendre un siècle ou un millénaire pour demander pardon à ces
[espèces?

Là, c'est un musée de la centrale électrique aux abords de la cascade;
on y fait l'éloge de ses multiples croquis.
Les pierres du fleuve mises à nu
poussent vers le ciel des soupirs feutrés.
Ô Soleil qui revêt le masque du chef
tout en écoutant aboyer le renard blanc. Les humains sont la mesure de toute
[la création.
Un nombre considérable de singes n'ont pas le droit de vote.
Les vérités prononcées par soi-même ne peuvent être prouvées que par les
[générations futures.
Il ne s'agit pas d'un retour au passé, ce sont plutôt les vies individuelles
qui se souviennent d'un esprit ayant péri.
C'est le silence que le moi sait offrir à la tradition,
et il n'appartient à aucune langue.
Il n'y a qu'une seule tare dans n'importe quelle langue:
c'est de décrire de la même façon différentes sortes de chagrins.
Les grappes de bâtiments en béton tridimensionnels sont comme des biens
[clonés,

ce sont les débris de la planète moderne;
pas de déjà-vu ici; ou plutôt, c'est le même visage.

Voici l'endroit futur conçu par l'imagination:

ils ont quitté ce lieu des milliers de fois, mais ils y
reviendront, car les esprits ancestraux y sont toujours.
On ne saurait dire s'il s'agit d'une responsabilité ou d'un devoir,
mais ils n'ont plus besoin de se fier à leur mémoire pour ouvrir l'ancienne
[porte en bois;
ce n'est qu'une ombre qui survit au fond des rêves.
Voici donc une ville intelligente.
Les générations suivantes ignorent totalement
le nom de ces villages de montagne. Si le narrateur
voulait les leur nommer, il n'aurait pas forcément la tâche facile.
Ici, les pâtés de maisons standardisés ont été scientifiquement planifiés,
et même la nourriture de base quotidienne ne diffère pratiquement pas.
Ce n'est pas le château de Kafka, mais pour les humains, c'est du pareil au
[même.
Les matériaux de construction sont comme des morceaux de cristal
[translucide,
et il ne reste aucun parfum du souffle de la terre et des quatre saisons.
Leur vie est complètement dominée par l'Internet,
aucun besoin de faits réels; quel que soit l'obstacle qu'ils traversent,
ils peuvent voir les yeux électroniques scintillants sur le dôme.
Plus besoin de se promener à cheval aux abords du canyon.
Le célèbre étalon, Dali Azong[1], ne survit que dans les pages du dictionnaire;

[1] Dali Azong est le nom d'un cheval célèbre dans l'histoire du peuple Yi.

il n'entendra pas les vivats lancés dans l'hippodrome circulaire.
À l'époque, cette race de chevaux de montagne n'était pas encore éteinte;
en plus de servir d'animaux de compagnie pour les enfants dans les zoos,
ils formaient une espèce digne de protection,
Qui sait de combien de louanges et d'honneurs ils ont fait l'objet!
D'innombrables guerriers ont gravé leur nom dans l'histoire grâce au
[dévouement de leurs chevaux.
L'existence du sellier fabriquant la selle tricolore a perdu sa valeur,
même si on conserve ses produits dans les musées de la ville,
et malgré l'admiration des touristes qui les voient; l'ère des chevaux
a pris fin, le halo des cavaliers s'est estompé,
et la prophétie qui voulait que l'on trouve le fer à cheval est insensée;
les salutations qu'envoient les pales des moulins à vent sur les montagnes
[lointaines
disent à une humanité qui vient de s'éveiller que cet âge a radicalement
[changé.
À l'époque, la navigation était plus rapide qu'aujourd'hui, mais tout le
monde peut aller n'importe où selon son bon vouloir grâce aux nouveaux
moyens de transport.
C'est une victoire pour la science, un triomphe de la technologie,
mais ce n'est en aucun cas une victoire totale pour l'humanité, puisque nous
[avons
perdu la dernière personne capable de chanter une berceuse en entier.

Ô terre promise où le verre est coulé par le temps qui passe,
ce n'est pas la saison des pluies d'été; du côté opposé, indéterminable,
les larmes et la pluie ont formé un axe central inséparable,
transformant les chaînes de montagnes escarpées en position de sommeil des
[amoureux,

et une puissante chanson folklorique au ton aigu nous émeut encore et encore;
ceux qui se sont éloignés de la tradition pour survivre dans le présent
ont oublié tout le sens accumulé dans les racines des mots.
Il n'y a pas de place pour un foyer dans la pièce; le feu tamisé
n'apparaît que dans les souvenirs des aînés qui peu à peu s'effacent.
De temps en temps, ces souvenirs se réveillent,
déposant des larmes boueuses au creux des rides foncées.
Ô, Flammes. C'est vous qui avez illuminé le centre de distribution
de la sagesse d'un millénaire, transmise de père en fils,
qui nous dit comment accueillir la vie et affronter la mort,
faire flotter les mots vifs de la langue maternelle dans un vide perpétuel.
Seule la lumière du feu fait en sorte que ceux qui se sont rassemblés
autour du cercle puissent voir clairement dans le noir.
Pourtant, en cette région de logements numérisés,
les besoins à combler ne diffèrent aucunement;
les gens abstraits domineront complètement le monde.
Dans les composites en acier et en béton
gît la future patrie façonnée par de nouveaux matériaux.
S'il y a encore narrateur qui vive, il regardera
de face le soleil roulant de cette façon
et il rendra hommage à tous les êtres vivants comme le faisaient ses ancêtres.
Maintenant sa voix est la seule présence,
et le squelette de son timbre est ce qui soutient l'horizon lumineux.
Par son invocation, il fera se déplacer les fleuves;
la solennité des montagnes transcende chaque instant.
Toute forme de vie, même celle de minuscules insectes,
rassemblera ses rangs
et se ruera pour faire partie d'une cérémonie en faveur de la vie.

L'invocateur d'aujourd'hui n'est pas un bimo[1].
C'est son appel qui s'est frayé son propre chemin
partant de ce château en maille tissée,
même si le chemin en question ne menait pas
à notre monde traditionnel en voie de disparition,
mais il nous a laissé voir les toit de l'architecture Chuandou[2] depuis
[longtemps disparus,
et la mythique cuillère en bois du géant.

Il y a un temple où l'électricité et les ascenseurs transportent les gens,
et de chaque fenêtre, c'est la même scène que l'on peut voir.
Le regard de l'aîné est tourné vers l'horizon terre de Sienne brûlée,
sombrant dans un état contemplatif profond, car il veut entendre
le gazouillis printanier des coucous.
Démêler les rides qui s'échappent dans le temps; seule la clé secrète de la
[guimbarde
peut dire les vicissitudes du destin et l'impermanence de la vie.
Un enfant voit sur son écran d'ordinateur des braconniers démembrer au
[pôle Nord
un dauphin, et les empreintes digitales de l'esprit des tueurs
teignent en rouge la feuille blanche posée sur son bureau.
Afin de subvenir aux besoins de ceux qui habitent encore la patrie de
[l'humanité,
leurs enfants ou leurs parents ont déjà travaillé sans relâche à travers tout le
[pays.
Ils ne peuvent que retourner dans cette soi-disant patrie ancestrale

---

[1] Les bimos sont les prêtres traditionnels du peuple Yi.

[2] Le style Chuandu est l'un des deux principaux systèmes de charpente de l'architecture traditionnelle chinoise. Le système Chuandou fait usage de piliers et de traverses.

à la fin de l'année, oh Dieu merci.
Mis à part les sommes d'argent qu'ils ont gagnées, ils ne peuvent qu'y
ramener le dialecte venant d'ailleurs.
Après les blagues, la langue maternelle se prend dans la gorge.
Il n'y a pas de trains à bord desquels ils ne veulent pas monter,
et les pistes monétaires permettent aux survivants de voyager n'importe où.
[Les pâtés
de maisons en trois dimensions, aux mesures fixes, sont déjà devenus la norme,
et d'imposants fils électriques relient des montagnes transparentes.
Le bourdonnement des machines résonne de loin,
la foule de l'emploi collectif se tient de l'autre côté du mur-rideau de verre,
les ombres des gens ordonnées comme des unités fixes.
Ô personnes vertueuses de cette planète,
même si vous travaillez dans différentes langues et êtes vêtus autrement,
vos cœurs peuvent-ils entrer au même moment
dans un tunnel illuminé de fond en comble par la justice et la vérité?
Qui pourrait croire que vous portez un jugement précis
entre deux arcs bruts de réalité;
pourquoi ne pas laisser les parties s'enfoncer dans tout le nombril,
et dire à plus de gens qu'il faut chercher un terrain d'entente.
Ces choses ténues sont un caillou, un bouton, un bout de papier,
et quand quelqu'un, encore et encore, vous souffle gentiment à oreille,
[continuellement,
le manteau porte-bonheur tombe du ciel,
et l'écuelle en bois perdue dans l'enfance apparaît comme par magie.

Les anciennes maisons aux toits de planches n'existent plus,
elles étaient les enfants des montagnes; la fumée blanche des cheminées
montant en spirale remplissait la terre et le ciel d'échelles rampantes.

C'était le silex du soleil qui de son ombre a réveillé
les membres magnétiques du clan lovés dans le bassin et l'abdomen des
[montagnes.
L'aigle plane toujours dans le vide paisible cherchant des traces de
[mouvement,
et la fourmi en fouillant le sol fait un bruit sensible.
Le royaume patate de la logique à une époque de famine,
la structure des atomes de sarrasin amer a sauvé les enfants d'un peuple.
L'origine des senteurs de maïs grillé dans les poèmes et légendes;
la vie mi-fermière, mi-bergère, fondement inaltérable des proverbes,
lorsque la sagesse largement partagée frappe à la porte du mystère.
Ce sont les flammes qui implorent auprès des gens
pour leur parler des rochers irrationnels cachés dans le langage.
Ô poivrons rouges incalculables, ô patrie des Nuosus[1],
avec vos écrans éblouissants vous comblez chaque façade
de peintures rouges interrompues au plus fort de l'automne.
Ah, montagnes, vallées et forêts faites de mots prononcés en plusieurs
[dialectes,
il est plus difficile de trouver ici un étranger qu'un membre de sa parenté.
Le joueur de guitaire lunaire portant un pantalon évasé cheville
qui chante sur la route de montagne, vêtu d'une cape de feutre.
Le coq aux plumes scintillantes qu'appelle la faisane juchée sur la crête.
La toison blanche comme neige qui s'entasse sur le sol au centre du village
durant la fête de la tonte.
Ah, le coq d'or que chaque garçon a élevé pendant son enfance.
Le concours de beauté du Festival de la Torche, les normes de beauté
[traditionnelles,

[1] Le peuple Yi qui habite le Liangshan se dénomme lui-même "Nuosu", terme qui signifie "peuple noir".

le cœur et les dehors ne font qu'un dans le flux de la lumière et de l'ombre.
Ah, les moutons noirs ayant suivi les migrations dans les épopées,
des milliers d'années durant.
Nous avons mastiqué les maximes au fond de nos gorges et de nos estomacs.
Sur cette terre, la réalité et les réflexions ont avalé l'absurde pour en faire des
vies de carnavals, complexes dans la glace du miroir.
Chaque nuit, la lumière du feu éclaire les aînés et les enfants,
ainsi que la timidité de la jeune femme; elle ricane, main sur la bouche,
les yeux remplis de rêves; ah, les ailes des oiseaux sur le point de prendre
[leur envol
entre la guimbarde et la guitare!
Accueillant une nouvelle vie pour la première fois l'ombre des flammes
laisse l'émerveillement de la lumière briller dans les pupilles du nourrisson.
Ô, accueillir la mort pour enfin porter un coup au festin de l'absurde.
L'abattage de leur bétail est chose sérieuse,
c'est ainsi qu'ils font leurs adieux ultimes à la mort et à la vie,
et aucune autre cérémonie ne pourrait le surpasser;
en gémissant ils font tomber d'autres animaux sous les pierres mortelles.
Le langage des cailloux et marteaux qui ne peuvent témoigner
de la résurrection des morts, c'est ici, et nulle part ailleurs,
qu'il peut goûter la valeur de la communauté pour un individu.
Châtiment ou rédemption, je l'ignore, mais le souffle de l'humanité moderne
monte et descend dans les couloirs vitrés comme du mercure,
les seins ne regorgent plus de lait mais d'horrible silicone
et la reproduction de la vie est confiée à des éprouvettes blanches.
Que les êtres chers reviennent frapper le berceau du corps céleste
comme des nourrissons, choisissant non seulement la langue maternelle
pour épancher leur esprit; parmi eux la partie centrale des montagnes,
le crâne que traverse notre esprit.

Oh, peut-être n'est-ce pas l'âge que nous imaginions,
car de moins en moins d'enfants peuvent réciter la généalogie des héros,
et qui sait diriger le chant des cortèges funèbres est devenu un oiseau rare.
Les plus grosses galettes de sarrasin au monde donnent un certain répit
aux plus vulnérables qui ont faim et à tous ceux qui sont dans le besoin.
Laissez les langues anciennes dans les lois les plus récentes
devenir les textes du monde.
Les mots suivent une pente naturelle, ils vous bénissent
de pierres incandescentes pour en dissiper la souillure.
Que ceux qui forent les peaux de vache soient ravis.
Les torches de pin sifflantes allumées, la réincarnation de mon père.
Montagnes de chaque côté des flancs, pentes abruptes de la terre penchée
vers la gauche, brasero d'Hétilaba [1] : la selle noire est un banquet réservé
[aux parures d'argent.
Descendants des Nuosus, si vous ne l'avez pas encore oublié,
offrez à l'occasion du Kushi [2] un pichet de vin salabo [3] aux esprits
[ancestraux;
ainsi les mains en charge du sacrifice ouvriront les entrailles du sel et de la
[liqueur!
Face au soleil éternel, criez, et saupoudrez des fragments d'or et d'argent!
Les pièces de monnaie des deux mondes s'emmêlent
à la ligne de partage entre la vie et la mort, les ombres du noir et blanc en

---

[1] Hétilaba est l'un des hommes forts des légendes du peuple Nuosu. Il a tué Ge're Abi, l'émissaire de l'empereur dépêché pour prélever les impôts, en allumant une torche afin de tuer les "insectes nuisibles". Les générations suivantes ont institué le Festival de la Torche pour commémorer cet événement.

[2] Kushi est le nom donné au Nouvel An en langue yi. Le Nouvel An du peuple Yi se fête autour du 20 décembre du calendrier grégorien.

[3] Le salabo est une ancienne cruche à vin qu'utilise le peuple Yi.

[copulant
s'égosillent en sentiments prolongés.
Seul l'oiseau de la branche divine garde pour lui la coupe d'argent.
Ce n'est pas un progrès absolu et ce n'est pas
non plus que d'être arriéré au sens moderne du terme.
Oh, tu as donné assez d'eau
mais tu as enlevé le peu de sel qu'il restait.
Sans les pompons rouges ornant l'agate de l'âme,
à quoi servent les plaques positives?

D'innombrables marches en béton inondées de soleil,
et on n'entend pas bêler ici les chèvres noires au loin,
leurs yeux couverts de poussière que soulèvent les troupeaux
en sautillant de haut en bas?
Les chèvres noires sont sacrifiées, indispensables au culte des ancêtres.
C'était alors un âge d'intelligence, les âmes des gens
vouées à s'attarder dans les canyons sans fin de la vie et de la mort,
pour ensuite retourner dans le désert chercher le tapis de mariage
de tous les êtres vivants,
grimper du plus bas de la falaise jusqu'aux endroits les plus hauts,
chutant, pratiquant la lutte, l'équitation, ces anciennes tournois.
Peut-être n'est-ce qu'en retournant aux organes du corps doré
que les fils de l'humanité pourront hisser les drapeaux
de la masculinité et de la créativité.
C'est la terre promise, cachée dans une autre dimension de l'univers;
elle n'existe pas réellement, elle est de l'ordre de l'inconnu,
un territoire abstrait et sans nom de la rivière du temps.
Montagnes, pieds nus, armure, sarrasin,

meules de foin, bols en cuir doré, guitares lunaire, mabu[1],
couteaux aux manches incrustés de bijoux, gobelets à griffes d'aigle,
piliers de pierre soutenant le pot, nœuds du héros, cire de miel,
mantra pour l'envoi de l'âme, feutre blanc,
vent de montagne, généalogie[2], proverbes, épopées,
amulettes, common law, âmes du purgatoire libérées, flammes, fusils,
noms liés du père et du fils, liqueur, cousines,
parenté consanguine, mariage, aigles sacrés,
sages, selles, parures, traditions,
Festival de la Torche, guerriers, lieux de crémation,
migration en toute liberté, dignité, défunts,
quiconque peut aller à la rencontre de la mort et vénère le noir, sincère,
[passionné,
animiste, prêteur de serment, intimement lié à la chair et au sang,
identité, reconnaissance, solennité, structure, vaillance.
Ils savent pourquoi les gens continuent à vivre:
se détacher de la queue que le néant rattache à la comète
n'est pas une superstition scientifique, les dieux contrôlent la divinité des
[humains,
et leurs prophéties, il n'y a que les gens qui d'habitude puissent les
confirmer.
C'est la terre promise, et la race humaine a besoin d'un certain temps
avant de pouvoir entrer dans sa gare à grande vitesse, transparente comme le
[jour.
Ces habitants sont les futurs descendants de cette race;

---

[1] Le mabu est un ancien instrument à vent du peuple Yi.

[2] Chez les Yi, le terme "généalogie" fait référence à l'arbre généalogique du clan. Tous les hommes Yi savent le réciter par cœur.

ils n'ont pas le choix car ils ne peuvent que gagner
le pouvoir de l'étonnement, de la sauvagerie et de la colère de leur propre
[réveil.
Ô terre promise, à cette époque
peut-être leur poète sera-t-il encore en vie; je crois fermement,
bien qu'il garde toujours, fixément, la même position en train de chanter,
que la torche qu'il tient dans la main illuminera le monde.

Si nous prétendons avoir déjà vu l'avenir,
nous sommes comme des frères jumeaux debout à la station du temps,
l'un face au ciel, l'autre face aux ténèbres,
et le monde devient alors très petit,
l'eau glacée de l'Arctique coule sur tout ton front, et au Sahara la lueur
du clair de lune tombe enceinte dans une valise.
Et ce jour-là se trouve être le moment d'accueillir et d'expulser les esprits
[ancestraux.
Ceux qui ne sont pas en vie sont assis là; quand la liqueur
dans l'écuelle en bois est portée aux lèvres, la foudre
qui apporte à la fois douleur et plaisir
couronne le bien de la nature humaine, permet au mal de commencer à
[mourir,
et quand elle naîtra, faisons de la bonté, désormais, la seule vertu.
Laissons les choses pitoyables aux soins de l'avenir, et ne soulevons pas la
[houe
pour leur nuire, car des milliers d'espèces
existent depuis des millions d'années au-delà des champs.
La douleur et les situations qu'elles ont vécues ne sont pas d'hier,
ce siècle surpasse largement le passé, et malheureusement,
la première chose qu'oublient les animaux, c'est le malheur qui les a frappés.

Que le temps s'étale vraiment en quatre dimensions, que les graines du bien
tombent une fois encore dans les entrailles, et que seuls les étoiles et
l'immuable soleil paternel démontrent ce que Russell a annoncé aux gens du
[futur.
Que différentes langues maternelles prennent vie dans l'arithmétique, car il
[existe
différentes façons de penser, mieux que le pragmatisme de la rationalité
[instrumentale.
Seul quand on ramènera la race humaine dans la contrée sauvage à la lueur
[des torches
et que chaque visage sera couvert de peinture à l'huile de bronze
les pas de danse Duoluohe [1] fouleront-ils les rythmes secrets de la terre,
et le drap rouge sur la tête du taureau proclamera-t-il la puissance de la nature
et le désir originel de l'homme à nouveau réunis dans la ruche tremblante.
Regagnez le lit conjugal de la terre! Faites en sorte que la fertilité des gens
pèse dans la balance, car c'est la fête de la vie, et bien sûr, c'est aussi la fête
[du peuple.

Ô terre promise, j'espère de tout cœur qu'à ce moment-là
les gens feront toujours partie de ce monde.

Françoise Roy
（弗朗索瓦丝·罗伊译）

[1] Le Duoluohe est une ancienne danse de groupe exécutée par les femmes Yi.

Das Verheißene Land

Schau, dort ist das verheißene Land!
Natürlich ist es nicht Jahwes Gabe an die Juden,
dort fließt keine weiße Milch.
Mag sein, es ist ein Stück künftiger Erde,
keinesfalls eine Utopie, vielmehr eine moderne Welt,
verschanzt zwischen den Flöten und Sphären der Tradition,
aus Glas und nichts als ein Ding der Form.
Die Distanz von Gestirn und Haupt bliebe da ohne Wandel,
weder nah noch fern unserer Seele.
Ach, Zeit, du hast geändert und beendet
die siebte Weise unseres Weges zur Unsterblichkeit.
Damals kreiste in den Lüften ein einziger Adler.
Seine Existenz allein war der dubiose Beweis
für den Sinn des Lebens.
Von oben auf die große Erde geschaut, ach, Gestirn!
Die schiefe Himmelsleiter trägt den Willen gebogenen Schirms,
das ist das Schachbrett des Geistes, der ölig graue Glanz,
kreuz und quer von den Autobahnen her aufleuchtend.
Das ist nicht der Weg heim, der Pfad der Vergangenheit
verlief sich beizeiten tief im Hirn des Vagabunden. Nie mehr
wird sein eines Knaben Flötenspiel, winkend in den Hügeln.
Die Spuren seiner Schafherde entschwanden längst im Gestern.
Nun spiegeln sich die Schluchten an zerrissenen Himmeln,
die Flüsse sind zerschnitten zu digitalen Würsten. Die Einheit der Welt.

Laß die zornigen Orkane des Julis mit ihrem unsteten Jammer
den schwer atmenden Ufern ins Gesicht brüllen.

Um Abbitte zu tun vor all den Spezies, bedarf es da
eines Jahrhunderts oder tausend Jahre?

Da ist das Museum für Kaskadenkraftwerke,
alle möglichen Entwürfe fanden Zustimmung.
Steine, vom Fluß freigelegt, seufzen still gen Himmel.
Ach, Sonne! Mit der Maske eines Häuptlings
lauschst du dem Heulen weißer Füchse. Der Mensch
ist das Maß aller Dinge. Affen haben selten Stimmrecht,
eine Wahrheit im Selbstgespräch wird erst die Nachwelt bestätigen.
Ohne Rückkehr in die Vergangenheit erinnert sich
individuelles Leben allein an enteilenden Geist.
Dies ist das Schweigen des Ich, gewährt der Tradition,
es gehört keiner Sprache an.
Alles Ungenügen der Sprache ist nur einer Art:
dieselbe Beschreibung ungleicher Trübsal,
eine Ansammlung dreidimensionaler Betonbauten, nicht anders als geklonte Produkte,
Treibgüter eines modernen Gestirns,
keine alte Bekanntschaft, vielmehr dasselbe Gesicht.

Dies ist das Land vorgestellter Zukunft:

Sie sind zigmal von hier fortgezogen, doch sie
werden wiederkommen, denn ihre Ahnen sind dort,
schwer zu sagen, ob aus Verantwortung oder aus Pflicht.

Sie bedürfen keiner Erinnerung, um die alte Holztür zu öffnen,
die ist nur ein Schatten, lebendig im Traum.
Dies ist eine smarte Stadt. Die Namen der Bergfesten
sind den Nachfahren längst fremd. Falls der Geschichtenerzähler
sie zu benennen gedenkt, so ist das keine einfach Sache.
Die hiesigen standardisierten Straßenviertel gehorchen wissenschaftlichem Plan,
selbst das tägliche Essen ist mehr oder minder dasselbe.
Dies ist nicht Kafkas Schloß, aber für das menschliche Wesen dasselbe.
Baumaterial ist Stück für Stück wie ein durchsichtiger Kristall,
kein Geruch bleibt vom Atem der Erde und der Jahreszeiten.
Ihr Leben wird gänzlich eingeteilt vom Internet,
Wahrheit tut nicht not, Hindernis um Hindernis überwunden
fixiert man das blinkende elektronische Auge auf gebogenem Schirm.
Kein Ritt mehr durch die Täler,
der Name stolzer Rappen eine Sache des Lexikons,
kein Jubel mehr zu hören vom Rund der Rennbahn,
als das Bergland sicher noch seine Pferde kannte.
Sie sind nicht allein Hätschelwesen für Kinder im Zoo,
sie bleiben weiter wert der Protektion als Spezies.
Wer weiß noch, wieviel Preis und Ruhm der ihre war,
wie viele Recken sich ihrer Gabe wegen einen Namen machten?
Der Fertiger dreifarbiger Sättel verlor den Wert seiner Existenz,
auch wenn seine Werke in städtischen Museen stehen.
Besucher schauen sie mit anerkennendem Blick. Dies ist
keine Ära des Pferdes, der Nimbus des Reiters schwand.
Die Suche nach Hufeisen ist nun ohne prophetischen Sinn.
Grüße, von fernem Bergkamm mit den Blättern herbeigeweht,
sagen der erwachten Menschheit, die Zeiten haben sich geändert.

Die Navigation damals wollte schneller sein als heute,
neue Verkehrsmittel bringen jedermann an jeden Ort.
Das ist der Sieg der Wissenschaft, das ist der Sieg der Technik,
aber keinesfalls der volle Sieg des Menschen, denn wir
haben verloren den letzten Meistersänger eines Wiegenliedes.

Ach! Das verheißene Land, es liegt an Glases Rande, geschaffen
durch die Zeit, es war nicht die Regenzeit des Sommers,
unbestimmbar auf der anderen Seite. Tränen und Regen bildeten
eine untrennliche Achse. Sie zwang wilde Berge in den Schlaf von
Liebenden.
Seitdem trifft eine hohe Volksweise wieder und wieder in Mark und Bein,
die Stromer, fern der Tradition, zu Zwecken der Gegenwart,
haben vergessen den umfassenden Sinn, niedergelegt im Wort.
Die Häuser sind ohne Feuerstelle, ein Feuerschein erscheint
nur den Alten in schwindender Erinnerung, beiläufig wachgerufen,
die dunklen Falten gefüllt von trüben Tränen.
Oh, Flamme! Der Sammelpunkt von tausend Jahren Weisheit
ward einst erleuchtet von dir, weitergereicht vom Vater auf den Sohn.
Wie das Leben empfangen, und wie dem Tod begegnen,
so daß Worte, frisch und lebendig in ewiger Leere treiben?
Allein des Feuers Glanz läßt Menschen sitzend im Kreis
lebendig erblicken all die Dinge in der Finsternis.
Doch in den digitalisierten Wohnvierteln
wird sonst nichts angeboten.
Der abstrakte Mensch regiert vollkommen die Welt.
In Wohnblocks aus Stahl und Beton
steht das künftige Heim, geschaffen aus neuen Materialien.
Falls es noch einen Erzähler gibt, werden seine Augen

die herbeirollende Sonne ehren wie einst
die Ahnen alle Phänomene.
Seine Stimme wäre momentan das einzige Sein,
der knöcherne Ton stützte den hellen Horizont,
sein Ruf bewegte die Flüsse,
der Ernst der Berge überträfe einen jeden Moment,
ein jedes Leben, winzig wie das der Insekten,
sammelte sich in den eigenen Rängen,
um eilig teilzuhaben an der Zeremonie für das Leben.
Der heutige Rufer ist kein Priester.
Sein Ruf fand seinen Weg von einem Schloß gesponnen im Netz,
auch wenn dieser Weg nicht führte zur verlorenen Welt der Tradition,
und doch hat er uns erblicken lassen die Himmel verstoßener Bauweisen
mitsamt dem Holzlöffel eines mythischen Riesen.

Dies ist ein Tempel, da Elektrizität und Fahrstuhl Gäste befördern,
von jedem Fenster schaut man dieselbe Szene.
Der Blick der Alten fällt auf den rot-braunen Horizont,
versinkt in Meditation. Die Sehnsucht gilt dem Ruf des Kuckucks
im Frühling, um zu glätten die Falten auf der Flucht in die Zeit.
Nur die Maultrommel mit dem geheimen Schlüssel mag dir nennen
die vielen Makel deines Schicksals, die Unstetigkeit menschlichen Lebens.
Kinder sehen im Internet Wilderer am Nordpol Delphine verstümmeln,
und das leere Blatt auf dem Schreibtisch ist rot von den Fingerabdrücken
der Schlächter. Zur Unterstützung der Hinterlassenen im Garten
der Menschheit sind lang schon ihre Söhne oder Eltern im ganzen Land
mit aller Kraft tätig. Nur zum Jahresende können sie zurückkehren
in ihre Heimat, genannt Land der Ahnen. Ach, dem Himmel sei Dank.
Sie bringen mit ihre Ersparnisse und einen fremden Dialekt,

nach Scherzen an der Tür bleibt die Muttersprache schluchzend im Hals.
Sie nehmen jeden Zug, die Wege des Geldes erlauben
den Lebenswilligen die Reise an jeden Ort.
Dies ist ein dreidimensionales Straßenviertel, die Norm
ward längst Modell, Kabel himmelhoch, es zieht sie
zu den durchsichtigen Gebirgen.
Das Brummen der Maschinen treibt von fern herbei,
Kollektive schuften an Glasfassaden,
ihre Schatten gleichen in Reih und Glied gefügten Installationen.
Ach, all diese ehrwürdigen Gestalten der Erde.
Auch wenn ihr dieselbe Sprache sprecht, dasselbe anzieht,
vermag eure Seele gleichzeitig betreten
den Tunnel, erleuchtet von Gerechtigkeit und Wahrheit?
Wer kann glauben, ihr fällt ein korrektes Urteil
zwischen zwei unfertigen Bögen der Realität?
Warum nicht die Teile in den Nabel gänzlich sinken lassen,
um noch mehr Menschen eine offene Sehweise zu benennen?
All jene schwachen Dinge sind nichts anderes als ein Kiesel,
ein Knopf, ein Blatt Briefpapier, wenn jemand zwitschert
an jemandes Ohr, wiederholt, fortgesetzt, gutmütig,
der Umhang des Glücks mag fallen vom Himmel,
die Holzschale der Kindheit wunderbar erscheinen vor Augen.

Jene alten Fliesenhäuser sind nicht mehr,
sie waren die Kinder der Berge, der weiß sich windende Rauch der Esse
schuf dem Himmel und der Erde Steigleitern die Fülle.
Die Stammesmitglieder, magnetisiert schlafend im Becken und im Schoß der Berge,
hat wachgerufen der Sonne Flintstein Schatten.

Der Adler erwartet weiter in den stillen Lüften Spuren von Bewegung,
eine Ameise wendet den Boden, empfindlich der Klang.
Das Kartoffelreich der Logik, in Zeiten des Hungers
rettete der Bau von Atomen im bitteren Buchweizen
die Säuglinge eines Stammes. Der Ursprung von Mais,
entfaltete geröstet wohligen Duft in Gedichten und Sagen.
Teils Bauer, teils Hirte, das Leben ward der währende Grund manchen
Sprichworts.
Wenn Weisheit von Mund zu Mund an das Tor der Rätsel klopft
oder die Flamme dank Disput einem jeden erklärt
all die riesigen Kiesel, irrational verborgen in der Sprache.
Unberechenbar roter Paprika, ach, Nuosu, Land der Frauen!
Du nutzt betörende Leinwände an jeder Außenmauer
für zig Serien rötester Herbste. Ach, all die Berge, Schluchten,
Wälder, geschaffen von all den Dialekten, hier,
wo sich eher ein Verwandter als ein Fremder finden läßt.
Der Spieler der Mondlaute im Filzumhang auf des Berges Pfaden
singend Liebeslieder, das Hosenbein aufgeschlagen.
Der Fasan, glänzend in seinem Gefieder, gerufen von der Fasanin
zum Bergkamm! Schurfest, die Schafswolle weißer als Schnee
gehäuft auf weitem Feld. Ach, der goldene Hahn,
von einem jeden Burschen zur Kindheit genährt.
Schönheitswahl zum Fackelfest, da werden im Fluß
von Licht und Schatten Seele und Erscheinung eines.
So das traditionelle Urteil für Schönheit. Ach, die Zucht schwarzer Schafe
von Weg zu Weg mit den Epen schon tausend Jahr! Wir beißen und
schlucken, ob Kehle oder Magen, Wort für Wort. In diesen Landen
verschlingen Wirklichkeit und Schatten Absurditäten,
sie wuchsen in den Spiegeln zu mannigfach karnevaleskem Leben.

Jeden Abend bescheint das Feuer Alte und Kinder.
Die Scheu der Mädchen, verstohlen das Lachen, träumerisch der Blick.
Ach, der Vogel Flügel zwischen Maultrommel und Mondlaute,
bereit zum Flug! Sie nehmen an das neue Leben, Schattenflammen
erstmalig hinterlassen kindlichen Pupillen ein Staunen für das Licht.
Ach, willkommen, lieber Tod, zum letzten Schlag gegen das Bankett des Absurden.
Das Schlachten von Vieh ist kein Spiel,
es ist eine Vollendung, ein Abschied von Leben und Tod,
kein Ritual steht darüber. Die Wehklage läßt andere Tiere und tödliche Steine stürzen.
Unmöglich vermag die Sprache der Kiesel und der Hämmer zu bezeugen
die Auferstehung der Toten, hier und nur hier läßt sich verstehen der Wert
der Gemeinschaft für das Individuum.
Weiß nicht, ob Strafe oder Sühne, die moderne Menschheit atmet
auf und ab in einem quecksilbergleich glasierten Korridor,
die Brust schwillt nicht wegen der Milch, Silikon ist der üble Grund,
und die Pflicht, Leben zu mehren, ist weißen Reagenzgläsern anvertraut.
Laßt die Blutsverwandten zurückkehren, wie Kinder die Wiege,
diesen Himmelskörper treten, nicht nur die Muttersprache wählen,
um sich auszuschütten, darunter das Subjekt der Berge, der Schädel
da der Geist weht. Ach, vielleicht ist auch dies das Zeitalter,
nicht erdacht von uns. Kinder sagen kaum mehr auf Heldenstammbäume.
Vorsänger in Prozessionszügen sind lang schon seltene Tiere!
Der größte Buchweizenfladen auf Erden schenkt den hungrig Schwachen
und den Hilfebedürftigen ein wenig Raum.
Laßt alte Sprachen in neuestem Gesetz
den Text der Welt werden!
In Sprachen gibt es organische Hänge, sie rühmen dich,

sie entfernen dank rotglühender Steine allen Schmutz.
Laß die Gerber sich freuen über die Maßen!
Die Kieferfackeln brennen und zischen, Vaters Inkarnation!
Die Berge, Rippen auf beiden Seiten, Abhänge, links zur Erde.
Gebirgszüge, eines Riesen Feuerstelle: Schwarze Sättel
sind ein Bankett, vereinbart vom Silberschmuck.
Enkel der Nuosu, falls ihr noch nicht vergessen habt,
zum neuen Jahr reicht den Ahnen einen guten Tropfen im Pokal,
in den Händen der Opfernden sind geöffnet, was Salz ist, was Wein.
Im Anblick der ewigen Sonne rufet, werft Gold und Silber in Stücken!
Die Gelder zweier Welten an der Grenze von Leben und Tod,
die Schatten von Schwarz und Weiß vereint,
röchelnd ineinander. Nur ein Vogel auf göttlichen Zweigen beläßt
den Silberpokal für sich selbst. Dies ist kein absoluter Fortschritt,
und auch kein Rückschritt im modernen Sinn!
Ach, ihr habt gegeben genügend Wasser,
nur genommen ein wenig Salz.
Und wenn die roten Bommel auf dem Achat der Seelen fehlen,
wofür da noch die eifrigen Teller?

Zahllose Betonstufen, von Sonnenstrahlen umhüllt,
hier hört niemand das Meckern der schwarzen Ziegen.
Ach, wessen Augen blockiert ein Staub, aufgewirbelt vom
Sprung der Ziegenherden aus der Höhe in die Tiefe?
Schwarze Ziegen sind unverzichtbar beim Ahnenopfer,
das war ein Zeitalter der Klugheit, die menschliche Seelen
waren verurteilt, weiter zu zaudern in den endlosen Tälern von Leben
und Tod. Sie würden noch heimkehren wollen ins Offene auf der Suche
nach den Loden für die frische Vermählung aller Dinge,

um vom steilen Grund zu steigen zum höchsten Ort,
Ringen, Kämpfen, Reiten, all die alten Ertüchtigungen,
vielleicht nur bei Rückkehr zu den Organen goldener Leiber
vermögen die Söhne der Menschheit die Fahne von Männlichkeit
und Kreation zu hissen. Dies ist das verheißene Land, verborgen
in einer weiteren Breite des Kosmos. Es kennt keine wirkliche Existenz,
es entspricht dem unbekannten, namenlosen, abstrakten Reich
des Flusses der Zeit. Berge, blanke Füße, Panzer, bitterer Buchweizen,
Steinmühlen, goldene Lederschalen, Mondlauten, Blasmusik,
verzierte Messer, Adlerkrallenbecher, Topfsteine,
Heldenknoten, Bienenwachs, Schrift zur Begleitung der Seelen,
weiße Loden, Wind von den Bergen, Stammbaum, Sprichwörter,
Epen, Talisman, Gewohnheitsrecht, Erlösung der Seelen, Flammen,
Gewehre, die Namen von Vater und Sohn, Schnaps, Cousinen,
Blutsverwandtschaft, Heiraten, göttliche Adler, Weise, Pferdesättel,
Aufputz, Tradition, Laternenfest, Krieger, Feuerhallen,
freie Migration, Würde, Tote, wer zu sterben bereit ist,
wer das Schwarze ehrt, wer innerlich ist, wer Leidenschaft spürt,
alle Dinge sind beseelt, wer durch Schwur sich bindet, wer
nahesteht dem Leiblichen, Rang und Identität, Würde, Muster und Mut.
All diese wissen den Grund, warum jemand weiterlebt,
das heißt, laß alle aufheben den Schwanz, dem Kometen vom Nichts
beigegeben. Dies ist kein wissenschaftlicher Aberglauben,
menschliche Wahrsagungen, da sind die Götter drumherum,
göttliche Prophezeiungen vermag oftmals nur der Mensch zu bestätigen.
Dies ist das verheißene Land, die Menschheit bedarf noch
einer gewissen Zeit, dann erst kann sie betreten eine
Hochgeschwindigkeitsstation, durchsichtig wie der Tag.
Die dortigen Bewohner sind die künftigen Enkel dieser Rasse.

Sie haben keine andere Wahl, denn sie können nur aus eigenem
Erwachen erlangen die Kraft von Bestürzung, Barbarei und Zorn.
Ach, das verheißene Land, wenn die Zeit kommt, werden ihre Dichter
vielleicht noch leben. Ich glaube wahrlich, selbst wenn sie
in festem Glied ihre Lieder singen, die Fackel in ihren Händen
wird die Welt dennoch erleuchten.

Falls es heißt, wir hätten jene Zukunft schon gesehen,
so ist das wie mit Zwillingsbrüdern an der Poststation der Zeit,
der eine Richtung Paradies, der andere Richtung Finsternis.
Die Welt aber würde schrumpfen in dem Moment,
das Eiswasser des Nordpols betropfte voll deine Stirn. Der Mond
über der Sahara würde schwanger im Handgepäck.
Und der Tag wäre die richtige Zeit, um die Ahnengeister
zu bewillkommnen und zu verabschieden. Es sind nicht
die Lebenden, die da im Kreise sitzen, wenn der Schnaps
in der Holzschale den Lippen zuteilwird, entstehen gleichzeitig
Blitze von Schmerz und Freude. Das Gute im menschlichen Wesen
krönen, so daß das Böse bei der Geburt vergeht, so daß das Gute
hernach zur einzigen Tugend wird. Laßt der Zukunft etwas
Bemitleidenswertes, greift nicht zur Hacke, um zu schaden
all den Arten, die außerhalb von Feld und Garten schon
ewig existierten. Pein und Umstände, auf die sie stießen,
sind nicht erst heute aufgetreten. Es ist nur so, daß dieses Jahrhundert
bei weitem übertrifft alles Vergangene, die Tiere aber vergessen leider
als erstes das Leiden ihrer eigenen Spezies. Laßt die Zeit wirklich
Möglichkeit werden in allen vier Richtungen, laßt den Samen
des Guten in des Menschen Gebärmutter zurückkehren, laßt,
was Russell den Künftigen sagte, von den Sternen am Himmel und

von der väterlich ewigen Sonne bestätigen. Laßt unterschiedliche
Muttersprachen ein neues Leben gewinnen in der Arithmetik.
Grund sind die verschiedenen Denkweisen, ist nicht der Pragmatismus
praktischer Vernunft. Nur wenn die Rassen der Menschheit
unter der Leitung der Fackeln ins Offene zurückkehren, und wenn
ein jeder im Gesicht die bronzefarbene Schminke aufträgt,
und wenn der Frauen Ringeltanz den geheimen Takt
der großen Erde schlägt, hat das rote Tuch auf dem Bullenschädel
verkündet die Macht der Natur und die Urbegierde des Menschen,
gemeinsam einmal mehr in dem Zittern eines Bienenkorbs.
Zurück zur Ehestatt der großen Erde! Auf daß menschliche Zeugungskraft
werde ein Teil der Bürde. Dies ist das Fest des Lebens und natürlich
ist dies das Fest des Menschen.

Ach, verheißenes Land, wenn diese Zeit kommt, möge der Mensch
noch ein Teil dieser Welt sein.

Wolfgang Kubin

（顾彬译）

La Terra Promessa

Guarda, ecco la terra promessa!
Non il dono annunciato dal Dio al popolo ebreo,
non il paese stillante di candido latte.
Forse un brandello di terra futura,
non un'altra Utopia, ma la modernità
fra il flauto della tradizione e la sfera
un mondo costrutto di vetro e prodotti di stampo.
Immutata la distanza tra gli astri e i nostri capi,
ora vicini ora lontani però dalle nostre anime,
oh! Tempo, hai mutato e concluso
il settimo percorso per l'eternità.
Sarà allora un'unica aquila a volteggiare in alto.
Esisterà, fornendo al significato della vita
una, opinabile prova.
Sporgiti dalle sommità a guardare la Terra, pianeta!
Scale inclinate a sorreggere volontà arcuate,
scacchiera delle capacità intellettive, reticolato
di autostrade scintillanti di grigi bagliori.
Non più la strada di casa, sentiero antico
impresso nel cranio dei vagabondi, non più

un bimbo che saluta suonando il piffero dal crinale,
tracce del suo gregge scomparse nel tempo di ieri.
La valle riflessi capovolti si proiettano sul cielo squarciato.
Il corso del fiume tranci di salsiccia digitale. Omogeneità del mondo.
Furiose tempeste del settimo mese con capricciosi
ululati, ruggiscono ai volti ansimanti sulle due sponde.

Dovremo attendere un secolo o un millennio perché chiedano venia alle
creature?

Museo della centrale idroelettrica a cascata
decantata per la varietà del disegno.
Pietre nude dal fiume inviano muti sospiri al cielo.
Oh, sole! Indossa la maschera del capo tribù
in ascolto dell'urlo della volpe bianca. L'uomo è misura dei diecimila esseri,
miriadi di scimmie non hanno diritto al voto,
soltanto i posteri forniranno prova del monologo della verità.
Non un desiderio di tornare al passato, ma una vita individuale
come anelito di spiriti andati.
Silenzio offerto dall'io alla tradizione,
non appartiene ad alcun linguaggio.
Comune pecca di ogni lingua,
parole uniche a narrare diversi dolori.
A grappoli di cemento si ergono i prodotti della clonazione,
relitti galleggianti sul pianeta odierno,
non dejà vu, ma identici volti.

Futuro luogo dell'immaginazione:

mille volte abbandonata, tuttavia
luogo delle anime degli avi, meta perenne,
per responsabilità o dovere, difficile dirlo.
Senza bisogno del ricordo per spingere la porta di legno,
ombra perenne presente nei sogni.
Nella città intelligente, "roccaforte" è parola
ignota ai posteri, se un narratore
vuole usarla, non sarebbe facile.
Quartieri dal tracciato modello frutto di progettazione scientifica,
quotidiani alimenti di base pressoché identici.
Non il castello di Kafka, ma per alcuni è come se lo fosse.
Materiali da costruzione frammenti di cristallo trasparente,
persi sono il sapore del fango e il respiro delle stagioni.
Esistenze dominate dalla rete,
fanno a meno della verità, ogni ostacolo si supera
sotto occhi elettronici che ammiccanti scrutano dal cielo.
Non serve un cavallo per solcare il canyon,
il celebre Dali'azong [1]
oramai relegato al dizionario,
più non si odono esultazioni nella giostra equestre,
al tempo i cavalli di montagna non erano ancora estinti,
ridotti a compagni per i bambini negli zoo,
ma meritevoli di salvaguardia,
chissà quanta gloria e ammirazione hanno ottenuto
innumerevoli eroi per merito loro immortalati nei libri di storia.
Artigiano della sella tricolore, priva della ragion d'essere,
seppur oggetto pregiato nei musei cittadini,

---

[1] Dali'azong, celebre destriero nella storia delpopolo Yi.

a suscitare ammirazione nei visitatori, non è
un tempo per cavalli, sbiadita è l'aura del cavaliere,
non ha senso cercare auspici nel ferro dello zoccolo,
da lontani crinali il vento fa mulinare auguri di foglie,
annuncio all'umanità appena desta, di immani mutamenti.
Il navigatore sarà più veloce, nuovi mezzi di trasporto
porteranno chiunque ovunque voglia.
Vittoria della scienza, della tecnologia,
non certo vittoria umana a tuttotondo, abbiamo
perso l'ultimo cantore di ninnenanne.

Oh! Terra promessa, oltre il vetro temperato dalle ore,
non c'è temporale estivo, sul retro incerto,
un asse inscindibile di lacrime e pioggia,
l'asperità dei monti addolcita in pose di amanti dormienti.
A perdifiato echeggia il canto popolare a rimescolare viscere,
gli svaghi avulsi dalla tradizione, per sopravvivere ai tempi
si è perso il significato insito nelle radici di parole.
Nella stanza è sparito il focolare della terra, balugina il fuoco
flebile nella memoria addolcita di anziani.
Quando d'un tratto si evocano le scene,
torbide lacrime colmano le rughe oscure.
Oh, fiamma! Raccogli e diffondi un millennio di saggezza
alla tua luce, il padre tramanda al figlio,
ad accogliere alla vita, a confrontarsi con la morte,
i freschi toni del linguaggio natio fluttuano perenni nel cielo,
solo coloro intorno alle fiamme
vedono con chiarezza ciò che l'oscurità avvolge.
Nella dimora digitale,

non si soddisfa il bisogno di diversità,
saranno entità astratte a guidare il mondo.
Tra ibridi in acciaio e cemento
nuovi materiali costruiranno il giardino di domani,
se esiste ancora un cantastorie, con occhi
rivolti al bagliore rutilante del sole
come i suoi avi renderà omaggio alle diecimila creature.
La sua voce unica presenza,
ossatura a sorreggere i limiti sfolgoranti del cielo,
quel richiamo, muove il fiume nel suo corso
i monti acquistano solennità insuperata,
ogni creatura vivente, persino gli infinitesimi insetti
si raccoglie in ranghi,
per affrettarsi alla cerimonia rivolta alla vita.
A convocarci oggi non è il *bimo* [1]
Ma un richiamo totale, nella fortezza intessuta dalla rete
ha scovato un percorso, non conduce
al mondo della tradizione ormai scomparso,
ci mostra travi e colonne l'antica struttura del cielo
e l'enorme cucchiaio di legno dei giganti del mito.

Nel tempio trasportato da energia ed elevatori,
identico panorama in ogni finestra,
lo sguardo degli anziani si proietta verso l'orizzonte cremisi,
sprofondati nei pensieri, in ascolto del cuculo a primavera,
a distendere le pieghe rifugiatesi nel tempo, il codice racchiuso nel *kouxian*
narra i risvolti del destino e l'impermanenza della vita.
Nei computer i bambini osservano i bracconieri al polo Nord

---

[1] *Bimo*, "maestro delle scritture" sacerdote delpopolo Yi.

squartare i delfini, sulla scrivania i fogli
recano tracce insanguinate dagli intenti dello sterminatore.
Per nutríre i custodi del giardino dell'umanità,
figli e genitori in questo Paese
si spargono ai quattro venti, riversano le energie nel lavoro.
Agli sgoccioli dell'anno tornano al cosiddetto
luogo degli avi, oh, cielo e terra vi ringrazio,
oltre ai risparmi portano linguaggi esotici,
dopo le battute si strozza in gola il saluto nella lingua natia.
Non c'è treno su cui non siano pronti a salire, sulle rotaie del denaro
per sopravvivere possono andare ovunque.
Quartieri tridimensionali, criteri standardizzati
resi paradigma, cavi svettanti infilano trasparenti collane di monti.
Da lontano giunge il ronzio delle macchine,
folle raccolte al lavoro oltre la vetrata,
silhouettes disposte in atteggiamenti cristallizzati.
Oh, uomini nobili, notabili del pianeta,
parlate lingue diverse, indossate abiti differenti,
potrebbero forse le vostre anime nello stesso attimo
entrare nel tunnel illuminato da senso morale, giustizia e verità?
Chi può credere che prendiate la giusta decisione,
tra due rozzi semicerchi di realtà,
perché non lasciare che una parte si deprima nell'onfalo del tutto,
trasmettere l'idea di accettare di dissentire,
fievoli elementi, una pietruzza, un bottone!
un foglio di carta da lettera, tra i mormorii assidui, ripetuti, bonari,
la mantella della fortuna scenderà dal cielo
la ciotola di legno perduta nell'infanzia riemergerà d'incanto.

Non più antiche case dal tetto di tegole,
figlie della montagna, bianche volute di fumo
a riempire cielo e terra di scale ascendenti.
Magnetici clan assopiti sui fianchi e nel ventre dei monti
si destano all'ombra della selce nel sole.
Il falco nel vuoto quieto scruta tracce di movimento,
il suono percettibile di una formica a rivoltare la terra.
Nel regno logico della patata, nell'era della fame
la struttura delle particelle di grano saraceno ha salvato i neonati del clan.
Origini del granturco, tostati effluvi in poesia e leggenda,
la vita agro-pastorale, base immutabile di proverbi,
saggezza diffusa a bussare alle porte dell'arcano
le fiamme argomentano narrazioni
di macigni irrazionali celati nel linguaggio.
Incalcolabile peperoncino rosso, ah, patria dei Nuosu!
Con accecante effetto cinematografico, su ogni muro di cinta
si appendono immagini di vermiglio rigoglio autunnale.
Ah, tra montagne, valli e foreste creazione di dialetti diversi,
è più arduo trovare estranei che familiari!
Tra i sentieri di montagna, le spalle coperte dalla mantella canta
accompagnandosi al *yueqin* il calzone dal piccolo orlo!
Il richiamo della femmina attira sul crinale il bagliore piumato del gallo
selvatico!
La festa della tosatura raccoglie sulla diga lana più candida della neve!
Ah, il gallo dorato compagno di infanzia di ogni bambino!
La gara della festa della torcia, tradizionale valutazione di bellezza
nel flusso di luci e ombre si fondono spirito e aspetto!
Ah, per migliaia di anni montoni neri si sono mossi al seguito dell'epica!
Massime masticate scendono in gola a raggiungere lo stomaco!

Su questa terra realtà e ombre divorato l'assurdo
si replicano in gioiose riflessioni allo specchio.
Ogni falò illumina la notte di giovani e vecchi,
ritrosia di giovinette, risolini celati dalla mano, occhi colmi di sogni,
ah, tra *kouxian* e *yueqin* ali di uccello, preparatevi al volo!
Accoglienza di nuove vite, per prime le ombre delle fiamme
accendono di meraviglia le pupille dei neonati.
Oh, nel ricevere la morte, il banchetto sferra l'ultimo colpo all'assurdo,
non uccidono bestie per gioco
ma per compiere il congedo tra vita e morte,
massima cerimonia tra le altre, i loro lamenti
spingono ogni altro animale a cadere insieme al masso fatale.
Non si assiste al dialogo tra la pietra della resurrezione e il martello
soltanto qui, unica occasione
di percepire il valore della comunità per il singolo.
Chissà se in punizione o redenzione, oggi l'umanità
è respiro fluttuante argento vivo nei passaggi di vetro,
le mammelle non gonfie di latte ma perverso silicone,
la riproduzione affidata a provette bianche.
Lascia che gli amati tornino, neonati a scalciare la culla del cielo,
la lingua natia non è solo per le confidenze, tra queste
il tema dei monti è spirito a toccare il cranio.
Oh, forse quell'era non è come l'avevamo immaginata,
sempre meno giovani recitano le genealogie degli eroi,
chi sa accompagnare i defunti con il canto
è ormai bestia rara!
La frittella di grano saraceno più grande della Terra, ai deboli affamati
e ai bisognosi di aiuto dona briciole di spazio,
lascia che il linguaggio antico nelle leggi attuali

diventi testo del mondo!
Tra le parole il pendio organico, lode a te
con pietre roventi elimini il lordume!
Lascia coloro infilati nella pelle di bue a ottenere felicità inaspettate!
Bagliori di pino sibilano bruciando, incarnazione dei padri!
I monti coste sui due lati, spiovente a sinistra,
la catena del braciere di Atilaba [1] ; sulla sella nera
orpelli argentati invitano al banchetto.
Discendenti dei Nuosu [2] , se non l'avete dimenticato
al Kushi [3] offrite nel tempio una brocca *salabo* [4] alle anime degli avi,
la mano del celebrante squarci le viscere al sale e al vino!
Al cospetto dell'eterno sole, richiamo, frammenti sparsi di ori e argenti!
Il denaro di due mondi,
ai confini tra vita e morte, nell'oscurità si accoppiano bianco e nero
con urla prolungate
l'uccello sul ramo magico riserva per sé la coppa d'argento!
Non è assoluto progresso, né
arretratezza in termini moderni!
Ah, avete offerto acqua a sufficienza
portando via quel poco di sale che c'era.

---

[1] Atilaba, uomo dalla forza prodigiosa che, nella leggenda del popolo Yi, ha sfidato nella lotta e ucciso Sireabi, inviato a riscuotere tributi. Quando le divinità infuriate punirono gli Yi con una invasione di cavallette, Atilaba costruì torce giganti per fermare la piaga. In memoria delle sue gesta, ogni anno si celebra la Festa della torcia.

[2] Nuosu, "popolo nero" è il nome con il quale una delle tribù Yi del monte Liang chiama se stessa.

[3] Kushi, "nuovo anno" , che il popolo Yi celebra intorno al venti dicembre.

[4] *Salabo*, antica brocca da vino.

Senza le nappe rosse sull'agata dell'anima
a cosa vi servirebbero piatti più generosi?

Trascale di cemento avviluppate da infiniti raggi di sole,
non si ode il belato delle capre nere,
ah, in lontananza, mandrie saltellano verso il basso
nubi di polvere a offuscare quali occhi?
La capra nera immancabile vittima nel sacrificio agli avi,
quella l'era dell'intelligenza, anime
predestinate esitanti sull'orlo dell'infinita valle di vita e morte,
a ritrovare la vita selvaggia, l'arazzo del connubio dei diecimila esseri.
Dall'ipogeo delle valli arrampicarsi fino in vetta,
lottatori, pugili, cavalieri, arti antiche,
forse solo recuperando organi creati in oro,
i figli dell'uomo produrranno stendardi di sublime virilità.
Questa è la terra promessa, celata in altra dimensione cosmica,
esistenza irreale, si oppone allo scorrere del tempo
ignoto e anonimo nella terra dell'astrazione.
Montagne, piedi nudi, corazze, grano saraceno,
macina, ciotola in pelle dorata, *yueqin*, *mabu* [1],
spada preziosa, coppa d'artiglio aquilino, pietra *guozhuang*,
nodo degli eroi, cera d'api, sentiero del ritorno delle anime, tappeto bianco,
brezza di montagna, *pudie* [2], massime, epica,
talismano, leggi non scritte, liberazione delle anime, fiamma, fucile,
patronimico, vino, cugina, linea di sangue, sensale, aquila sacra,
saggio, sella, ornamenti,
tradizione, festa della torcia, guerriero, luogo della cremazione,

[1] *Mabu*, antico strumento musicale.
[2] *Pudie*, genealogia del popolo Yi. Tutti i maschi la sanno recitare.

libera migrazione, dignità, morti,
volontà di morte, sublimità del nero, introverso, affettuoso,
ogni creatura ha un'anima, giuramento, sangue del tuo sangue,
identità, assimilazione, solennità, struttura, prodezze.
Sanno i motivi per continuare a vivere,
come evitare la coda vuota aggiunta alla cometa,
non è superstizione scientifica, gli dei disegnano i destini dell'uomo,
le loro premonizioni si confermano solo negli uomini.
Questa è la terra promessa, un attimo prima che l'umanità
entri nella stazione ad alta velocità trasparente come il giorno.
Gli abitanti, eredi del futuro della razza,
non hanno altra scelta, soltanto
di trarre dal risveglio una forza stupita, selvaggia e furente.
Ah, la terra promessa, in quel momento,
forse i poeti saranno ancora vivi, nella convinzione
seppur immobili sul posto,
reggano la torcia che illumina il mondo.

Se diciamo di aver visto il futuro,
si tratta di due gemelli nella stazione di posta del tempo,
uno rivolto verso il paradiso, l'altro confronta l'oscurità,
in quell'attimo il mondo minuscolo
i ghiacci del polo Nord a bagnarti la fronte, nel deserto del Sahara
la luce lunare s'ingravida in valigia.
È momento di accoglienza e di congedo dalle anime ancestrali.
Non sono i vivi a sedere in cerchio, quando la ciotola di legno
porta il vino alle labbra, il lampo che insieme nutre dolore e felicità,
incorona la carità umana, quando il male affiora
inizia già a morire, lasciamo che sia la bontà unica morale,

come patetico lascito al futuro, non usiamo la zappa
per non danneggiarli, in mille, cento forme le cose
esistono da milioni di anni al di là dei campi.
Dolore e destino, non sono prerogativa dell'ora
ma in questa era hanno superato ogni precedente, per nostra sfortuna
gli animali sono i primi a dimenticare la sciagura dei simili.
Lascia sia il tempo tra le quattro dimensioni a diventare reale possibilità, i semi della bontà
tornino all'utero, delle parole di Russell agli uomini del futuro
l'esattezza è confermata dagli astri in cielo e dal sole eterno padre.
Lingue diverse rinascono nell'arte del calcolo, differenti modi di pensare,
attratta dalle torce l'umanità torna alla prateria,
i visi di ognuno traboccano di antichi riflessi bronzati,
i passi del Duoluohe [1] battono il ritmo segreto della Terra, drappi rossi sul muso delle mucche
annunciano rinnovati incontri in nidi tremuli tra forze della natura e desiderio primordiale dell'uomo.
Torna al talamo della Terra! La fertilità diventi parte del peso,
è la festa della vita, certo anche dell'umanità.

Ah, terra promessa, se soltanto arrivati a quel momento gli uomini
potessero condividere quel mondo.

Patrizia Liberati

（李莎译）

[1] Duoluohe, antica danza di gruppo rappresentata dalle donne del popolo Yi.

Tierra Prometida

Verás, he aquí la tierra prometida.
No es, por supuesto, el regalo que el Señor prometió a los judíos;
ahí no fluyen ríos de leche blanca.
Podría ser una tierra futura,
no necesariamente otra utopía,
sino un mundo de vidrio y productos moldeados
diseñado por la era moderna
entre flautas y esferas tradicionales.
Allí, no ha cambiado la distancia entre las estrellas y nuestras cabezas,
pero las estrellas parecen ora cercanas, ora lejanas.
Oh tiempo, has cambiado y acabado
con el séptimo camino rumbo a la eternidad.
En aquel entonces, la única águila aún volaba en las alturas.
Su existir significaba que el sentido de la vida
venía de pruebas dudosas.
La tierra mirada desde la cúspide, oh Planeta.
La escalera inclinada soporta el peso de la cúpula en su determinación.
Es el tablero de ajedrez donde juegan las capacidades de la mente;
las autopistas entrecruzadas brillan con un gris lustroso.

No son los caminos de regreso a casa; los senderos de antaño
han desaparecido en la base del cráneo del vagabundo, nunca más habrá
un niño tocando flauta dulce en las colinas, moviendo las manos.
Su rebaño de ovejas desapareció en el ayer.
El reflejo del cañón se derrama hacia el cielo fracturado.
Han cortado los ríos en salchichas de números.
La uniformidad del mundo.
Los gritos erráticos y lúgubres de las trombas de julio, con su llanto incesante
y caprichoso rugen ante los rostros jadeantes en ambas orillas del río.

¿Tenemos acaso que esperar un siglo o un milenio para disculparnos ante
aquellas especies?

He aquí el museo de la central eléctrica construida en unas cataratas;
se ha elogiado por sus variados diseños.
Las piedras de los ríos al descubierto
devuelven silenciosos suspiros hacia el cielo.
Oh Sol, tú que llevas la máscara del cacique
que escucha los gritos del zorro blanco. El ser humano es la medida de toda
la creación.
Un número considerable de monos no tienen el derecho de voto.
Las verdades autoproclamadas solo pueden ser probadas por las generaciones
futuras.
Esto no significa un regreso al pasado, es la vida individual
recordando un espíritu que pereció.
Es el silencio que brinda el yo a la tradición,
y no pertenece a ningún idioma.
No hay sino un solo tipo de deficiencia en cualquier idioma:
describir de manera idéntica las penas de distinta índole.
Los edificios de hormigón tridimensionales en racimos son como bienes

clonados,
son los residuos flotantes del planeta moderno; no es deja vu sino más bien
la misma cara.

He aquí el futuro lugar que imaginamos:

han dejado este lugar miles de veces, pero
volverán, porque los espíritus ancestrales todavía están allí.
No se puede decir con certeza si se trata de una responsabilidad o un deber.
Ya no necesitan confiar en su memoria para abrir la vieja puerta de madera;
no es más que una sombra que pervive en los sueños.
Esta es una ciudad inteligente.
Las siguientes generaciones desconocerán por completo,
el nombre impostor. Si el narrador
quiere decírselo, no le resultará necesariamente fácil.
Las manzanas de la ciudad estandarizadas aquí han sido planificadas
científicamente,
incluso la alimentación básica de todos los días es prácticamente la misma.
Sin ser el castillo de Kafka, para los humanos es la misma cosa.
Los materiales de construcción son como piezas de cristal translúcido,
ya no huelen el aliento de la tierra al respirar, ni el de las cuatro estaciones.
Sus vidas están completamente dominadas por el Internet.
y no hacen falta hechos reales; en cualquier obstáculo que superen,
pueden ver las cámaras de tráfico parpadear en la cúpula.
No más paseos a lomo de caballo por el cañón.
El famoso caballo, Dali Azong, no sobrevive más que en el diccionario;
no escuchará los vítores en la pista de carreras.
En aquel entonces, todavía existían esos caballos de montaña;
además de ser mascotas para los niños en el zoológico,

eran una especie digna de protección.
Quién sabe cuántas alabanzas y honores recibieron:
innumerables guerreros han pasado a la historia por la dedicación de sus caballos.
El que exista el fabricante de sillas tricolor es algo que ha perdido su valor,
aunque existan sus productos en los museos de la ciudad
y los turistas los miren con admiración; esta no es
la era de los caballos, el halo de los jinetes se ha desvanecido,
y buscar la profecía de la herradura ya no tiene sentido.
Los saludos que envían las aspas de los molinos de viento en las montañas lejanas
le dicen a una humanidad recién despierta que esta era ha cambiado por completo.
En aquel entonces, la navegación era más rápida que la actual, pero los nuevos
medios de transporte pueden llevar a cada uno a cualquier lugar de su antojo.
Es una victoria para la ciencia, una victoria para la tecnología,
pero de ninguna manera una victoria cabal para la humanidad, ya que
hemos perdido a la última persona capaz de entonar una canción de cuna completa.

Oh tierra prometida por el cristal que ha fundido el tiempo.
no es el temporal de verano; en el lado opuesto, indeterminable,
las lágrimas y la lluvia formaron un eje central inseparable,
convirtiendo agrestes montañas en posiciones de amantes dormidos,
y una poderosa canción popular en voz cada vez más atiplada nos conmueve;
quienes se han alejado de la tradición para sobrevivir en el presente
han olvidado todo el significado que encierran las raíces de las palabras.
No hay lugar en la habitación para el horno; el fuego tenue

solo aparece en los recuerdos de los ancianos, que lentamente se erosionan.
De vez en cuando afloran los recuerdos, llenando las arrugas oscuras
de lágrimas fangosas.
Ay, llamas. Iluminaron ustedes el núcleo de distribución
de la sabiduría correspondiente a un milenio, transmitida de padres a hijos,
que enseña cómo acoger la vida y afrontar la muerte,
haciendo flotar las palabras vivas de la lengua materna en el vacío eterno.
Solo la luz del fuego puede hacer que quienes estén reunidos
alrededor del círculo vean claramente en la oscuridad.
Sin embargo, en esta región de viviendas digitalizadas,
lo que se puede brindar no son necesidades personalizadas.
los pueblos abstractos dominarán el mundo enteramente.
En conglomerados de acero y hormigón
está la futura patria modelada por nuevos materiales.
Si todavía hay un narrador que viva, su mirar
se enfrentará al sol que rueda por aquí,
rindiendo homenaje a todos los seres vivos como lo hacían sus antepasados.
Ahora su voz es la única presencia,
y el esqueleto de su timbre sostiene el horizonte luminoso.
Con su invocación, conmoverá los ríos
porque la solemnidad de las montañas trasciende cada momento.
Todas las formas de vida, incluso la de los insectos diminutos, cerrarán filas,
apresurándose para ser parte de una ceremonia a favor de la vida.
El invocador de hoy en día no es un bimo.
Es más bien su llamada la que encontró camino
a partir de este castillo de malla tejida,
aunque este no conduzca
a nuestro mundo tradicional en peligro de extinción,
pero nos dejó ver los cielos de la arquitectura Chuandou desaparecidos hace

mucho,
y la mítica cuchara de madera del gigante.

Es un templo sostenido por electricidad y ascensores,
y desde cada ventana se puede ver la misma escena.
Se volvió hacia el horizonte siena tostado la mirada del anciano,
que se absorbe en profunda contemplación, pues quiere oír
el trino primaveral del cuco.
Para desenredar las arrugas refugiadas en el tiempo, solo los códigos secretos
del birimbao pueden decirte las vicisitudes del destino y la impermanencia
de la vida.
En la pantalla de su computadora, un niño ve a cazadores furtivos
desmembrar
en el Polo Norte un delfín, y las huellas dactilares de los espíritus asesinos
pintan de rojo la hoja en blanco puesta en el escritorio.
Para apoyar a los que siguen habitando la patria de la humanidad,
hijos o padres ya trabajan incansablemente por todo el país.
Solo pueden regresar a esta supuesta patria ancestral
al final del año, ay, a Dios gracias.
Aparte del dinero que han juntado,
solo pueden traer de vuelta el dialecto de otro lugar.
Después de las bromas, el saludo de la lengua materna se atasca en la
garganta.
No hay trenes que ellos no quieran tomar, pues
los rieles de dinero permiten sobrevivir y viajar a cualquier parte.
Esta es una manzana urbana tridimensional y las normas estandarizadas
pasaron ya a ser un molde universal; imponentes cables eléctricos
conectan montañas transparentes.
Se puede escuchar el zumbido de las máquinas a lo lejos,

la multitud del empleo colectivo está del otro lado del muro-cortina de cristal,
y sus sombras son ordenadas como unidades fijas.
Oh gente virtuosa de este planeta,
incluso si trabajan en diferentes idiomas y se visten de manera distinta,
¿pueden sus corazones entrar al mismo tiempo
en un túnel completamente iluminado por la justicia y la verdad?
¿Quién creerá que pueden rendir un juicio acertado
entre dos arcos crudos de la realidad?;
¿por qué no dejar que las partes se hundan en el ombligo del todo?
y decir a más personas cómo encontrar puntos en común salvando diferencias?
Estas cosas endebles son un guijarro, un botón, un trozo de papel,
cuando alguien constantemente te susurra al oído, continua y bondadosamente,
el poncho de la suerte caerá del cielo,
y el cuenco de madera perdido en la infancia mágicamente aparecerá.

Las antiguas casas con techos de teja ya no existen,
eran las hijas de las montañas; el humo blanco de chimenea
elevándose en espiral llenó la tierra y el cielo con escaleras rampantes.
Fue la sombra del pedernal del sol la que despertó
a los miembros del clan magnéticos, dormidos en la pelvis y el vientre de las montañas.
El águila sigue buscando en el vacío silencioso señales de movimiento,
y la hormiga hurga en el suelo, haciendo un ruido sensible.
En el reino de la patata de la lógica en tiempos de hambruna,
la estructura de los átomos del trigo sarraceno amargo salvó a los hijos de un pueblo.

El origen del maíz despide un olor a tostado en los poemas y las leyendas;
la vida mitad labrador, mitad pastor, fundamento inalterable de los proverbios,
cuando el recitar la sabiduría llama a la puerta del misterio,
son las llamas las que con alegatos le habla al pueblo
de los peñascos irracionales escondidos en el lenguaje.
Los pimientos rojos en número incalculable, oh patria nuosu
usan pantallas deslumbrantes para llenar cada una de las fachadas
de continuas pinturas rojas en la cúspide del otoño.
Ah, montañas, valles y bosques hechos de palabras en diferentes dialectos,
es más difícil encontrar allí a un extraño que a un pariente.
El que toca el yueqin, esa harpa de luna,
y lleva pantalones tobilleros
entonando canciones de amor en el sendero de montaña vistiendo capa de fieltro.
El gallo de plumas brillantes al que llama en la cresta la hembra del faisán.
El vellón blanco como la nieve que se amontona en la plaza del pueblo
durante las fiestas de la esquila.
Ah, el gallo de color dorado que todo niño ha criado en su infancia.
El concurso de belleza del Festival de la Antorcha, los criterios de belleza tradicionales,
el corazón y la apariencia externa se vuelven una sola cosa en el flujo de luz y sombra.
Ah, las negras ovejas de cría que durante miles de años
han migrado al seguir las epopeyas.
Masticamos las máximas tragadas en nuestras gargantas y estómagos.
En esta tierra la realidad y las sombras han engullido lo absurdo y en el espejo,
se han convertido en vidas plurales, vidas de carnaval.

En cada noche en que la luz del fuego brilla sobre los ancianos y los niños,
la timidez de la jovencita; la risa furtiva, con la mano en la boca
y los ojos llenos de escenas oníricas; ¡ah, las alas de las aves entre el birimbao
y el yueqin están a punto de echar a volar!
Recibiendo la nueva vida, por primera vez las sombras de las llamas
dejan asombro por la luz en las pupilas del infante.
Oh, acoger la muerte para acabar atacando el festín de lo absurdo.
Proceder a la matanza de su ganado deja de ser para ellos un juego,
el adiós que realiza la muerte de la vida,
y ninguna otra ceremonia puede superarla,
sus gemidos hacen caer a otros animales con las piedras mortales.
El lenguaje de guijarros y martillos que no pueden ser testigos
de la resurrección de los muertos,
solo aquí, y en ningún otro lugar,
puede percibir el valor de la comunidad para un individuo.
Castigo o redención, no lo sé, pero el aliento de la humanidad moderna sube y baja
en pasillos acristalados como columna de mercurio,
los senos no se hinchan porque rebosen de leche sino de horrible silicona,
y la reproducción de la vida queda encomendada a probetas blancas.
Que los seres queridos regresen y pateen la cuna del cuerpo celestial como infantes,
eligiendo la lengua materna no solo para desahogar su mente; entre ellos
está el meollo de las montañas, el cráneo adonde se dirige nuestra mente.
Oh, tal vez no sea esta la edad que imaginamos,
y cada vez menos niños sepan recitar la genealogía de los héroes:
aquellos que pueden dirigir el canto de las procesiones fúnebres se han convertido

en bestias raras.
Los pasteles de trigo sarraceno más grandes del mundo alimentan a los débiles
que están hambrientos
y dan un respiro a los necesitados.
Dejen que las lenguas antiguas en las leyes más nuevas
se conviertan en los textos del mundo.
Las pendientes orgánicas de las palabras te bendicen,
¡disipan la suciedad con piedras fundidas al rojo vivo!
Que los que pasen por debajo del cuero de toro tengan una agradable sorpresa.
Las antorchas de pino silbantes en llamas, la reencarnación de mi padre.
Las montañas a ambos lados de las costillas, las escarpadas laderas de la tierra
inclinada hacia la izquierda, la montaña de Hetilaba, estanque de fuego: la silla negra
es un banquete reservado por los adornos de plata. Los descendientes nuosus,
si no lo han olvidado, dan a los espíritus ancestrales una jarra de vino salabo durante
el Kushi, ¡y las manos de quien hace sacrificios abrirán las entrañas de la sal
y de los licores!
¡Frente al sol eterno, llama y rocía fragmentos de oro y plata!
Las monedas de los dos mundos
entre la línea divisoria entre vida y muerte, las sombras del negro y del blanco
copulando se desgañitan en una estela de sentimientos.
Solo el ave de la rama divina se queda con la copa de plata.
No es progreso absoluto y tampoco es
un atraso en el sentido moderno de la palabra.

Oh, has dado suficiente agua
pero te has llevado la poca sal que había.
Sin las borlas rojas del ágata del alma,
¿para qué sirven las fuentes más activas?

Hay innumerables escalones de cemento bañados en la luz del sol,
pero aquí no se oye el balido de las cabras negras.
Oh, ¿qué ojos en la distancia están cubiertos del polvo
que levantan los rebaños de cabras cuando estas saltan desde lo alto?
Las cabras negras son sacrificio indispensable en el culto a los antepasados.
Era una época inteligente: las almas de las personas
estaban destinadas a vacilar entre ir adelante o atrás
en los interminables cañones de la vida y la muerte,
y volverían al campo abierto a buscar la alfombra nupcial de todos los seres vivientes,
subiendo desde lo más bajo del acantilado hasta los lugares más altos,
cayendo, practicando la lucha libre, montando a caballo, compitiendo
en esos viejos torneos.
Quizá sea solo volviendo a los órganos del cuerpo dorado
que los hijos de la humanidad podrán enarbolar las banderas de la masculinidad
y de la creatividad.
He aquí la tierra prometida, escondida en otra latitud del universo;
No es una existencia real, corresponde a lo desconocido,
un territorio abstracto y sin nombre del río temporal.
Montañas, gente descalza, armaduras, trigo sarraceno,
Molino de piedra, cuencos de cuero dorado, yueqines, mabu,
cuchillo del tesoro, copas de garra de águila, pilares de piedra que sostienen la vasija.

Nudos del héroe, cera de miel, mantra para el envío del alma, fieltro blanco,
viento de montaña, genealogía, proverbios, epopeyas,
amuletos, ley consuetudinaria, liberar almas del purgatorio,
llamas, pistolas, nombres vinculados de padre e hijo, licor, primas,
parientes consanguíneos, matrimonio, águilas sagradas,
sabios, sillas de montar, vestimenta,
tradiciones, Festival de la Antorcha, guerreros, campos de cremación,
migrar libremente, dignidad, muertos,
Quienes tiene el valor de encarar la muerte
y veneran el color negro, y son sinceros, apasionados,
animistas, que hacen juramentos, intiman con la carne y la sangre,
identidad, reconocimiento, solemnidad, perspectiva, valentía.
Ellos saben por qué la gente sigue viviendo:
para desprenderse de la cauda que la nada añade al cometa,
no es una superstición científica, pues la adivinación de los pueblos, son las deidades quienes la controlan,
y por lo general, las únicas que pueden confirmar las profecías de las deidades son las personas.
He aquí la tierra prometida, y la raza humana necesita algo de tiempo
para poder entrar en su estación de alta velocidad, transparente como el día.
Esos habitantes son los futuros descendientes de esta raza;
no tienen otra opción porque solo pueden adquirir
el poder del asombro, el salvajismo y la ira de su propio despertar.
Oh tierra prometida, en ese tiempo
su poeta aún podría estar vivo; yo creo firmemente,
aunque siempre esté de pie en una posición fija y aunque cante
la antorcha en su mano iluminará el mundo.

Si decimos que ya hemos visto ese futuro,

como hermanos gemelos en la estación del tiempo,
uno de cara al cielo, el otro de cara a la oscuridad,
y entonces el mundo se vuelve muy pequeño,
el agua helada del Ártico corre por tu frente, el claro de luna
en el Sahara queda embarazada en una maleta.
Y ese día es precisamente cuando hay que acoger y despedir
a los espíritus ancestrales.
No solo los vivos están sentados allí en círculo; cuando el licor
en el fondo del cuenco de madera llega a los labios, un rayo
que trae al mismo tiempo dolor y placer
corona el bien en la naturaleza humana. Deja entonces que el mal comience a morir
al momento de nacer, deja que la bondad sea en adelante la única virtud
y las cosas lamentables, deja unas cosas lamentables para el futuro,
y no uses la azada
para hacerles daño porque las diversas especies variopintas
han existido durante millones de años más allá de los campos.
El pesar y las situaciones por las que han pasado no son nuevos,
es solo que en este siglo han sobrepasado por mucho los del pasado,
y desafortunadamente, lo primero que olvidan los animales
son las desgracias que a sus congéneres les han sucedido.
Deja que una vez más regresen a la matriz de la humanidad,
que las estrellas y el eterno sol paterno demuestren
lo que Russell predijo a la gente del futuro.
Y que distintas lenguas maternas renazcan en la aritmética, por sus diferentes formas
de pensar en lugar de doblegarse ante el pragmatismo de la racionalidad instrumental.
Solo cuando la raza humana sea devuelta a la naturaleza iluminada por el

fuego de las antorchas
y cuando cada rostro esté cubierto de bronce oxidado
hollarán los pasos del baile Duoluohe los ritmos secretos de la tierra,
y el trapo rojo en la cabeza del toro proclamará que el poder de la naturaleza
y el deseo primitivo del hombre volvieron a unirse en la temblorosa colmena.
¡Vuelvan al tálamo de la tierra! Incluyan en el peso la fertilidad de la gente:
también es la celebración de la humanidad, y por supuesto, también es la
celebración del pueblo.

Oh tierra prometida, espero que en ese tiempo
las personas sigan siendo parte de este mundo.

Françoise Roy
（弗朗索瓦丝·罗伊译）

Förlovat Land

Titta där borta ligger det förlovade landet.
Såklart inte Guds löfte givet till judarna;
ingen vit mjölk flödar längs gatorna.
Det kan vara en framtida plats,
inte nödvändigtvis en annan utopi,
snarare en värld av glas och gjutjärn
moderna konstruktioner
bland traditionella flöjter och himlavalv
Där har inte avståndet mellan stjärnorna och våra huvuden förändrats,
utan stjärnorna tycks både nära och långt bort.
Å tid, du har förändrat och stängt
vår sjunde väg mot evigheten.
Då svävade den ensamma örnen fortfarande högt.
Att den fanns betydde att livets mening
fick ett osäkert bevis.
Å, att se ner på jorden, planeten, från dess högsta punkt.
Den lutande stegen bär upp kupolens beslutsamhet.
Den är sinnets möjligheters schackbräde; rutnätets
motorvägar glittrar i grå glans.

Den är inte vägen hem; det förflutnas smala stigar
har försvunnit in i vandrarens nacke, aldrig mer
spelar ett barn flöjt på kullarna, viftar med armarna i luften.
Hans fårflock försvann för länge sedan.
Flodbädden i ravinen speglar mot en fragmentarisk himmel.
Floden har skurits ner till digital hackfärs. Världen är likadan.
Juliregnen stormar oberäkneligt fram i sorg skriker
mot ansiktena som andas ansträngt på båda sidor om floden.

Väntar vi hundra eller tusen år innan vi ber dessa varelser om ursäkt?

Titta, där ligger ett vattenkraftsmuseum
som hyllar de många olika kraftverken.
De blottade flodstenarna
svarar himlen med tysta suckar.
Å, solen iklär sig hövdings mask
lyssnar till den vita rävens rop. Människan är alltings måttstock.
En avsevärd mängd apor utan rösträtt.
Egna sanningar kan bara bevisas av senare generationer.
Det här är inte att återvända till det förflutna, det är den enskilda
som minns en ande som skingrats.
Det här är tystnaden varje jag själv erbjuder traditionen,
den tillhör inget enskilt språk.
Det finns bara en brist gemensam i alla språk:
de erbjuder samma beskrivningar av olika sorger.
Ansamlingarna av betongbyggnader är som kloner,
den moderna planetens spillror;
inte som en deja vu; snarare är de ett och samma ansikte.

Så här föreställer vi oss framtiden:

De har lämnat den här platsen tusentals gånger, men de
kommer att återvända, eftersom förfädernas andar finns kvar där.
Oklart om det är för att ta ansvar eller av plikt.
De behöver inte längre lita på minnet för att öppna den uråldriga
träporten;
bara en skugga överlever i drömmen.
Detta är en uppkopplad stad.
Bergsbyarnas namn
är helt okända för kommande generationer. Om berättaren
vill berätta om dem kommer det inte att vara lätt.
De standardiserade kvarteren är planerade med linjal och vetenskap,
till och med vardagsmaten är exakt likadan för alla.
Detta är inte Kafkas Slott, men upplevelsen är samma för människorna i
det.
Allt byggnadsmaterial liknar klarglas
det finns inga dofter kvar, varken från jorden eller de fyra årstiderna.
Allas liv domineras fullständigt av uppkopplingen,
det finns inget behov av verklighet; oavsett vad människorna gör
kan de se de flimrande elektriska ögonen i kupolen.
Det finns inte längre någon anledning att rida längs flodbädden i
ravinen.
Den legendariska hästen Dalie-azho överlever bara i ordlistorna;
den kommer inte att höra hejaropen på tävlingsbanan.
Då var bergshästarna ännu inte utdöda;
förutom att barn kunde klappa dem på zoo
var de en art med värde nog att skyddas.
Vem vet hur de prisades och ärades,

oräkneliga krigares namn har bevarats i historien genom sina hästars
hängivenhet.
Sadelmakaren och den trefärgade sadeln har förlorat allt värde,
även om hans hantverk förvaras på museum,
och turister beundrar det; detta är inte
hästens tidsålder, ryttarnas sken har bleknat,
profetian om att finna en hästsko är meningslös;
väderkvarnarnas hälsningar från avlägsna berg
berättar för en nyvaken mänsklighet att tiderna har förändrats drastiskt.
Då hittade vi snabbare än vi gör i dag, nya transportmedel
kan föra vemsomhelst varsomhelst.
Det här är en vetenskapens seger och teknikens,
men på intet sätt en seger för hela mänskligheten, eftersom vi
förlorat den sista människan som kan sjunga en vaggvisa.

Å förlovade land där glaset gjuts av tid,
det är inte sommarens regnsäsong; på den vaga andra sidan
har regn och tårar förts samman till en enda droppe
som slipar bergskedjor efter de älskandes sovställningar,
en intensiv folksång berör oss om och om igen;
de som gått hän från traditionen för att överleva samtiden
har glömt den mening som finns i ett ords rötter.
Det finns inte längre plats för en eldstad i rummet; dunkel eld
finns bara i de långsamt tynande minnena hos de äldre.
Då och då väcks dessa minnen
och tårar rinner längs mörka rynkor.
Å flamma, visdom sedan tusentals år kommer från dig
i ditt sällskap delades den mellan far och son,
hur livet ska levas och döden mötas,

du får modersmålets levande ord att sväva under en evig tomhet.
Bara de som samlas i cirkel runt eldens ljus
kan se tydligt i mörkret.
Ändå, här på den här digitala platsen,
möts inga behov;
helt abstrakta människor dominerar världen.
Dess byggstenar är stål och betong,
det är framtidens hemland som gjutits av nya material.
Om berättaren fortfarande lever, kommer hans ögon
att möta solen som stiger närmre
och hedra allt levande så som hans förfäder gjort.
Numera finns bara hans röst kvar,
klangfärgens skelett håller ihop den lysande horisonten.
Hans besvärjelser rör floderna;
bergens höghet överskrider varje enskilt ögonblick.
Varje liv, till och med små insekter,
kommer att samlas
och ta del av denna ceremoni över livet.
Dagens besvärjare är inte en bimo. Det var hans sånger som hittade en
stig
bort från det här slottet av metallväv,
även om inte stigen leder
till vår försvinnande urvärld,
låter han oss få syn på en horisont av chuandou-byggda tak
som närapå försvunnit liksom den mytiska jättens träsked.

I detta tempel förflyttas människor med elektricitet och hissar,
här syns samma utsikt från varje fönster.
Förfaderns blick möter den tegelbruna horisonten,

försjunker i djupa tankar eftersom han längtar efter gökens vårsång
för att nysta upp rynkorna som flyr bort i tiden; munharpans hemlighet
är det enda som kan berätta om ödets skiftningar och livets
förgänglighet.
Ett barn ser på en dator hur tjuvjägare på Nordpolen
lemlästar en delfin, och det vita pappret på skrivbordet
har färgats rött av de rinnande fingeravtryck mördarnas tankar lämnat
efter sig.
För att ge stöd åt de som lever kvar i människans hemland,
har barn eller föräldrar arbetat oförtröttligt över hela landet.
De kan bara återvända till det så kallade förfäderliga hemlandet
vid årets slut, gudskelov.
Förutom pengarna de tjänat
kan de bara ta med sig dialekter från andra platser
och efter att de har skämtat lite fastnar modersmålet i strupen.
Det finns inga tåg de inte vill färdas med,
valutatågen får de överlevande att resa överallt.
Detta är ett kvadratiskt kvarter med en och samma standard
för allt och alla, höga stolpar med elektriska kablar kopplar samman
genomskinliga berg.
Hummandet från maskinerna hörs över långa avstånd,
arbetsstyrkans kollektiv finns på andra sidan glaskupan,
deras skuggor är ordnade i raka led.
Å planetens alla duktiga människor,
även om ni jobbar med olika språk och bär olika kläder,
kan era hjärtan på en och samma gång
gå in i en tunnel fullt upplyst av rättvisa och sanning?
Vem kan tro att ni kan välja rätt
mellan två oskrivna verkligheter;

varför inte låta alla delar samlas i samma navel,
berätta för fler människor om sökandet efter något gemensamt.
Ett grus, en knapp, en bit papper är svaga ting,
när någon igen och igen viskar vänligt i ditt öra
kommer lyckans slöja att falla från himlen,
barndomens försvunna träskål framträder igen, helt magiskt.

De uråldriga husen med trätäckta tak finns inte längre kvar,
de var bergens barn; vit skorstensrök steg som en spiral,
fyllde jorden och himlen med spiralformade takstegar.
Det var skuggan från solens flinta som väckte
de sammanfogade klansbröder som sov i bergets bäcken och mage.
Örnen är fortfarande i den stilla avgrunden på jakt efter spår av rörelse,
myran stökar runt i jorden, ger ifrån sig ett försiktigt ljud.
Potatiskejsardömet var bara logiskt under den stora svälten,
den bittra bovetens inre struktur räddade ett folks spädbarn.
Den rostade majsens ursprung i dikter och legender;
bonde-herdelivet, den oföränderliga grunden för ordspråk,
när så en vida känd visdom knackar på mysteriets dörr,
så är det flammor som vädjar till folket
de vill berätta om de irrationella stenblocken dolda inuti språken.
Oräkneliga röda peppar, å nosufolkets hemland.
Bländande fyller skärmar varje fasad
med oavbrutna röda målningar när hösten tar höjd.
Å berg, dalar, skogar sammanställda av ord från olika dialekter,
det är svårare att hitta en främling här än en släkting.
Månlutespelaren står i knälånga byxor
sjunger på bergsvägen iklädd en filtmantel.
Tuppen med gnistrande fjädrar blir uppropad på bergsryggen av

fasanhönan.
Ull vitare än snö staplad på bytorget under fårklippningsfesten.
Å den gyllene tuppen som alla pojkar tog hand om under sin barndom.
Skönhetstävlingen under fackelfestivalen, dess ursprungliga skönhetsideal,
hjärta och utseende samlas till ett i ett flöde av ljus och mörker.
Å det svarta fåret som följt berättelsernas folkvandringar över tusentals år.
Vi har tuggat sönder de livsråd vi svalt med hull och hår.
På dessa marker har verklighet och spegelbild svalt det absurda
och genom spegeln förvandlats till komplicerade karnevaler.

Varje natt lyser eldens ljus över åldermännen, barnen och
de unga kvinnornas blygd; hon fnissar och täcker sin mun
med ögon fyllda av drömmar;
å fåglarnas vingar mellan munharpan och månlutan lyfter snart!

Efter att ha fått ett nytt liv ger flammornas skuggor för första gången
ett ljusets förundran i spädbarnets pupiller.
Å välkomna döden att slå sitt sista slag på det absurdas festival.
Deras boskapsslakt är ingen lek,
den fulländar ett farväl till döden och livet,
ingen annan ceremoni är viktigare,
deras rop får de andra djuren att falla ihop av de dödliga stenarna.
Grusets och hammarens språk kan inte bevittna de dödas återuppståndelse
här, och bara här,
kan individen uppleva kollektivets värde.
Jag vet inte om det är straff eller försoning, den moderna mänsklighetens

andetag stiger och sjunker i kvicksilverglänsande korridorer,
bröstkorgar sväller, inte av mjölk utan från fruktansvärt silikon
och livets mirakel sker i vita provrör.
Låt de älskade bli spädbarn och välta den gudomliga kroppens vagga,
de väljer modersmålet för att tömma sina sinnen; bland dessa
är de flesta från bergen, som uppfyller våra sinnen.
Å kanske är detta inte den tid vi föreställt oss,
allt färre barn kan återberätta hjältarnas stamträd
och de som kan leda sången i begravningsföljen är numera sällsynta.
Världens största bovetekakor ger föda åt de svaga som är hungriga
och de som behöver lite hjälp får lite andrum.
Låt de uråldriga språken i de nyaste formerna
bli världens texter.
Ord har en självklar höjd, som välsignar dig
med rödglödgade renande stenar.
Låt de som borrar i kohudarna vara överlyckliga.
Tallstickan väser av eldsflammorna, min faders reinkarnation.
Berg på revbenens bägge sidor, till vänster lutar jordens branta stup,
festivalens hjälte Hetilabas eldgrop:
den svarta sadeln är en bjudning reserverad åt silverornament.
Ni som härstammar från nosu, om ni inte har glömt hur
ge förfadersandarna en salabo med vin under nyåret kushi,
och händerna som offrar kommer att öppna saltets och spritens
innanmäte!
Med ansiktet mot den eviga solen, ropa och strössla med flagor av guld
och silver!
De två världarnas mynt är sammanförda
vid gränsen mellan liv och död, vita och svarta skuggor i samlag
förlöser skrikande alla kvardröjande känslor.

Bara den gudomliga grenens fågel behåller silverkärlet för sig själv.
Detta är inte ständig tillväxt och det är inte
bakåtsträvande på något modernt sätt.
Å du har gett tillräckligt med vatten
men tagit allt salt som fanns däri.
Utan de röda tofsar som pryder andens agat
till vilken nytta är då all positivitet?

Bland oräkneliga betongsteg iklädda solljus;
går det bara att höra svarta getters bräkande
på avstånd, när getflockar, vars ögon är täckta av
virvlande damm, kastar sig ut från väldiga höjder?
Svarta getter är ovärderliga offer till förfäderna.
Det var en intelligensens tidsålder, människornas andar
var ödesbestämda att dröja kvar bland livets och dödens ändlösa raviner,
och de återvände till vildmarken för att söka efter allt levandes
bröllopsmatta,
att klättra från bergets lägsta punkt till dess högsta,
kasta sig utför, brottas, rida på hästar, alla dessa uråldriga tävlingar,
kanske kan mänsklighetens söner, bara genom att återlämna de inre
organen
till den gyllene kroppen, hissa maskulinitetens och kreativitetens flagg.
Det här är det förlovade landet, dolt i en annan dimension i universum;
det finns inte på riktigt, det talar bara med de okända,
abstrakta, namnlösa markerna som är tidens flod.
Berg, bara fötter, rustning, bovete,
slipstenar, gyllene läderskålar, månlutor, vindinstrumentet mabu,
ädelstensinfattade knivar, örnklobägare, stenpelare som håller grytan
ovan marken,

hjälteknutar för håret, bivax, mantrat som används för att skicka de
dödas andar vidare, vit
ullfilt, bergsvind, genealogi, ordspråk, hjälteberättelser,
amuletter, folklag, att befria andar från helvetet, eld, gevär,
fäders och söners sammankopplade namn, sprit, kvinnliga kusiner,
blodsband, släktingar, giftermål, heliga örnar,
visa män, sadlar, kläden,
traditioner, fackelfestivalen som hedrar Hetilaba, krigare,
kremeringsplatser,
fri rörlighet för människor, värdighet, de döda,
de som kan möta döden, vördar svart, innerliga, passionerade,
animistiska, edsvärande, intima med kött och blod,
identitet, igenkännande, högtidlighet, struktur, mod.
De vet varför människor fortsätter att leva:
att bryta sig fri från svansen som inte ger någonting till kometen,
det här är inte vetenskaplig vidskepelse, människors förutsägelser
kontrolleras av gudarna,
och gudarnas profetior kan oftast bara bekräftas av människor.
Det här är det förlovade landet, mänskligheten behöver lite tid
innan den, klar som en himmel, kan gå in i sin snabbtågsstation.
Dessa invånare är mänsklighetens framtids efterkommande;
de har inget annat val, då de bara kan förvärva
förvåningens, barbariets och ilskans kraft från det egna uppvaknandet.
Å förlovade land, vid den tidpunkten
kan deras poet fortfarande vara vid liv; jag tror fullt ut att
även om han fortfarande bara står i en enda position och sjunger,
kommer facklan i hans hand att lysa upp världen.

Om vi säger att vi redan sett framtiden,

den är som tvillingsyskon på tidens hållplats,
en som blickar mot himlen och en mot mörkret,
och världen blir liten i samma ögonblick,
arktiskt vatten faller över din panna, Sahara
ditt månljus blir havande i en resväska.
Och den dagen råkar vara dagen då det är dags att välkomna och skicka
iväg förfädersandar.
De som inte lever sitter häromkring; när spriten
i träskålen förs till läpparna, en blixt
som ger lika delar smärta och njutning,
kröner det goda hos mänskligheten, då ska ondskan dö
när den föds, godhet ska från och med i dag vara den enda dygden
och lämna ytterst lite åt framtiden, använd inte en hacka
för att skada de tusentals arter
som har funnits i miljoner år bortom åkrarna.
Smärtan och händelserna de upplever började inte i dag
men de senaste hundra åren har överträffat det förflutna, och olyckligtvis
glömmer djuren först av allt hur illa det gått för den egna arten.
Låt tid vara verkligt möjlig i fyra dimensioner, låt godhetens frö
återvända till fler människors livmödrar, låt det Russell sa till framtiden
bevisas med stjärnorna och den eviga solen som vittnen.
Låt olika modersmål livas upp av aritmetik, eftersom olika sätt att tänka
är bättre
utan rationalitetens instrumentella pragmatism.
Bara när mänskligheten leds tillbaka till vildmarkerna av facklor
och varje ansikte strålar av brons
kommer Dulohxodansen stega över jordens hemliga rytm
och det röda skynket över tjurens huvud utropa att naturens kraft
och människans ursprungliga åtrå återigen har förenats i en darrande

bikupa.
Återvänd till jordens äktenskapliga säng! Låt människors fruktbarhet bära all vikt,
detta är livets festival, och såklart är det en folkets festival.

Å förlovade land, jag hoppas att människor
fortfarande är del av världen då.

Freke Räihä
（弗雷克·赖海译）

Tărâmul Făgăduinței

Priviți, acolo este Tărâmul Făgăduinței!
Nu este darul promis de Dumnezeu pentru evrei, desigur,
Acolo nu curge lapte.
Acesta poate fi un loc al viitorului,
Nu o altă utopie, ceva modern,
O lume de sticlă și mulaje
Construită între fluturi și sfere tradiționale.
Acolo distanța dintre stea și capul nostru nu s-a schimbat,
Dar este atât de aproape de sufletul nostru
Ah! Timp, tu ai schimbat
Și ai încheiat
Cel de-al șaptelea nostru drum către eternitate.
Pe vremea aceea singurul vultur încă plutea sus.
Din cauza existenței sale, sensul vieții
Primește niște dovezi suspecte.
Din cel mai înalt loc cu vedere la pământ,
Ah, planetă!
Scările înclinate poartă voința domului,
Acolo e tabla de șah a funcțiilor minții,

Autostrăzile care se încrucişează emană
O lumină cenuşie, lucioasă.
Nu acesta este drumul spre casă, cărarea
De pe vremuri a fost ascunsă la baza craniului rătăcitorului,
Copilul care cânta la flaut şi făcea cu mâna
Din vârful dealului, nu mai există, urmele turmei sale
Au dispărut de mult, de ieri.
Imaginea inversă a defileului se suceşte spre cerul spart.
Fluviul este divizat în bucăţi de cârnaţi. Identitatea lumii.
Ploaia torenţială furioasă a lunii iulie
Să urle cu vaiete capricioase către
Feţele care gem de ambele maluri ale strâmtorii.

Cer scuze acestor specii, vor s-aştepte un secol, un mileniu?

Acolo e muzeul centralei electrice,
Oamenii laudă diferitele modele.
Pietrele goale ale râului oftează tăcut către cer.
Ah, soare! Cu masca de şefi, ascultă
Vuietul vulpii albe. Omul este măsura tuturor lucrurilor.
Un număr considerabil de maimuţe nu au drept de vot,
Adevărul vorbirii cu sine şi pentru sine
Poate fi dovedit numai de generaţiile ulterioare.
Nu există întoarce-n trecut, e doar amintirea
Vieţii individuale a spiritului pierdut.
Aceasta este tăcerea dăruirii de sine tradiţiei,
Ea nu aparţine nici unei limbi.
Există o singură insuficienţă a oricărui limbaj şi anume
De a descrie diferite dureri în acelaşi mod.

Grupurile de clădiri tridimensionale
Din beton sunt ca produsele clonate,
Acestea sunt obiectele plutitoare ale actualei planete,
Nu e ceva necunoscut, ci același chip.

Acesta este locul viitorului imaginat:

Au plecat de aici de mii de ori, dar se vor întoarce
Pentru că strămoșii sunt încă acolo și nu este clar
Dacă e vorba de vreo responsabilitate sau obligație.
Nu este nevoie să deschizi ușa stăveche
Bazându-te pe memorie. E doar o umbră, un vis.
Acesta este un oraș inteligent, numele satului de munte
E necunoscut generațiilor ulterioare. Nici naratorului
Nu i-ar fi ușor, chiar dac-ar vrea să-l spună.

Cvartalul standard de aici a fost planificat științific
Chiar și hrana de bază a fiecărei zile
Se stabilește în mod similar.
Acesta nu este castelul lui Kafka, dar
Pentru om, natura e la fel.
Materialele de construcție
Sunt bucăți de cristale transparente,
Fără miros de pământ și respirația celor patru anotimpuri.
Viețile lor sunt complet calculate de internet,
Nu e nevoie de dovezi, trec orice obstacol
Pe clădirile înalte se văd ochii electronici.
Gata cu călăria în jurul defileului,

Faimosul cal Dali Azong [1] supraviețuiește doar în dicționar
Ah, nu veți auzi urale pe hipodromul rotund,
Caii aceia de munte pe-atunci n-ar fi dispărut,
Fiind doar animal de companie al copiilor din grădina zoologică.
Desigur, ar fi o specie demnă de protecție
Cine știe câte laude și onoruri a primit,
Nenumărați războinici au rămas în istorie datorită dăruirii sale.
Producătorii de șei tricolore și-au pierdut valoarea existenței,
Chiar dacă capodoperele lor sunt păstrate în muzee urbane,
Turiștii în vizită au priviri admirative, acum nu mai este
O epocă a cailor, aureola călărețului a slăbit,
Profeția găsirii potcoavei nu are sens,
Salutări de la paletele rotative ale energiei eoliene de pe
Creastele îndepărtate ale munților,
Spune-le ființelor umane care tocmai s-au trezit:
Vremurile s-au schimbat dramatic.
Navigația pe atunci ar fi mai rapidă
Decât în prezent, mijloace de transport noi
Te pot duce oriunde vrei să mergi.
Aceasta este victoria științei, victoria tehnologiei,
Dar în niciun caz nu înseamnă victoria totală a omului,
Noi am pierdut ultima persoană care putea să cânte
Un cântec de leagăn în întregime.

Ah! Tărâm al Făgăduinței, dincolo de paharul timpului,
Nu sezonul ploios al verii, pe opusul nedeterminat,
Lacrimile și ploaia formează o axă inseparabilă,
Transformă munții aspri într-o poziție de dormit pentru un cuplu.

---

[1] Dali Azong, numele unui cal faimos din istoria etniei Yi.

Un cântec popular înalt a fost cântat în mod repetat,
Acei rătăcitori care sunt departe de tradiție,
Pentru supraviețuirea prezentului
Înțelesul complet al rădăcinii cuvintelor a fost uitat.
Nu există loc pentru o vatră în cameră, un foc slab
Apare doar în amintirile învechite treptat ale bătrânilor.
O astfel de scenă va fi trezită din întâmplare,
Ridurile întunecate erau pline de lacrimi noroioase.
Ah, flacără! Centrul de distribuție a o mie de ani de înțelepciune
Luminat de tine, învățat din tată în fiu,
Cum să întâlnești viața și cum să înfrunți moartea,
Lasă cuvintele vii ale limbii materne să plutească în golul etern,
Doar lumina focului îi poate face pe cei care stau în jur
Să vadă cu adevărat acele lucruri în întuneric.
Cu toate acestea, în această zonă de locuit digitală,
Ceea ce poate fi furnizat nu este o cerere diferită,
Oamenii abstracți vor domina complet lumea.
În amestecul de oţel şi ciment
Aceasta este viitoarea casă modelată de materiale noi,
Dacă naratorul trăiește, ochii lui
Se vor confrunta cu soarele venit de-a rostogolul
Omagiu tuturor lucrurilor ca și strămoșii săi.
Vocea lui este singura prezență în acest moment,
Scheletul calității sunetului susține cerul luminos,
Din cauza chemării sale, râul va fi mutat
Solemnitatea munților întrece orice clipă,
Fiecare viață, chiar și acea insectă minusculă este
În stare să-și adune propria echipă,
Grăbindu-se la o ceremonie pregătită doar pentru viață.

Invocatorul de astăzi nu este Bimo[1]
Aceea era chemarea lui, de la acest castel țesut
A găsit o cale, chiar dacă nu duce la
Lumea tradițională pe care-am pierdut-o,
Dar ne-a lăsat să vedem universul ceresc
Și lingura de lemn a uriașului mitic.

Acesta este templul alimentat de electricitate și ascensoare,
De la fiecare fereastră se vede aceeași scenă,
Ochii bătrânului s-au îndreptat spre orizontul ocru,
Căzând în contemplație, vreau să ascult
Cântecul cucului, primăvara,
Pentru a dezlega faldurile timpului de evadare,
Doar cu muzicuța îți poate vorbi
Despre destinul nefericit și despre impermanența vieții.
Copiii urmăresc braconierii din Arctica pe computer, dar și
Dezmembrarea delfinilor, în timp ce hârtia goală de pe birou
E pătată cu roșu de amprentele minții ucigașului.
Pentru a-i hrăni pe cei lăsați în urmă în patrie,
Copilul lor sau părintele lor este deja pretutindeni
În această țară, muncind din greu pentru un loc de muncă.
Abia la sfârșitul anului pot reveni în satul natal,
Pe pământul strămoșesc, slavă Domnului,
Ei aduc banii pe care i-au acumulat, limba unui pământ străin,
Salutul în limba maternă se îneacă-n gât, după vorbele amuzante.
Calea banilor le permite supraviețuitorilor
Să călătorească oriunde
Nu există tren pe care să nu-l poată lua.

[1] Bimo, preot în societatea tradițională a etniei Yi.

Acesta este cartier tridimensional, liniile directoare normative
Au devenit tipare, cablurile falnice
Sunt conectate cu munții transparenți.
Zumzetul mașinilor vine de la distanță,
Iar mulțimea angajaților este de cealaltă parte
A peretelui cortină de sticlă,
Umbrele lor sunt ordonate ca niște instalații fixe.

Ah, oameni virtuoși de pe această planetă,
Pot inimile voastre să intre în același moment
Într-un tunel complet iluminat de moralitate și adevăr,
În ciuda limbilor voastre diferite și a ținutelor diferite?
Cine poate crede că veți face o judecată dreaptă,
Între cele două arce neprelucrate ale realității,
De ce nu lăsați partea să se cufunde în buricul întregului,
De ce nu spuneți tuturor calea căutării unui teren comun
Cei slabi sunt o piatră, un nasture, o coală de scris,
Când cineva șoptește la ureche,
În mod repetat, continuu și cu blândețe,
Pelerina norocului va scădea din cer, iar bolul
Pierdut în copilărie va apărea magic în fața ochilor.

Acele case vechi de țiglă nu mai există,
Ele erau copiii munților, iar fumul alb, în valuri,
Umplea cerul și pământul cu scări aievea.
Tribul magnetic care dormea în văile și-n burta munților
Erau treziți de umbra de cremene a soarelui.
Vulturul încă urmărește amprentele în mișcare în golul liniștit,
Iar o furnică întoarce solul cu un icnet ușor.

Logica regatului cartofului, structura atomului de hrişcă
Au salvat bebeluşii de întreaga rasă în epoca înfometării.
Izvorul porumbului, aromele dulciurilor
Din poezii şi din legende,
Viaţa pe jumătate de fermă şi pe jumătate păstorească,
Temeiul inalterabil al proverbelor,
Când cântecele înţelepciunii băteau la uşa misterului,
Erau flăcările care le grăiau tuturor argumentat, despre
Acei bolovani iraţionali ascunşi în limbaj.
Ardei roşii incalculabili,
Ah, grădina Nuosu!
Fiecare perete exterior se acoperea orbitor
În sezonul de vârf al toamnei, cu grupuri de picturi roşii.
Ah, munţi, văi şi păduri de cuvinte în diferite dialecte,
Erau mai greu de găsit străinii decât rudele!
Muzicanţii la chitara lunii,
Cu pelerine pe umeri şi pantaloni cu manşete înguste,
Cântau melodii de dragoste pe drumul de munte!
Chemarea cocoşului cu pene sclipitoare pe creasta muntelui
La strigarea fazanului!
Festivalul de tuns oile, cu grămezi de lână pe baraj,
Mai albă decât zăpada!
Ah, cocoşul mare de aur hrănit în copilărie de orice băiat!
La concursul de frumuseţe al Festivalului Torţei,
Evaluarea tradiţională a frumuseţii asupra minţii şi înfăţişării socotită laolaltă
În fluxul de lumină şi umbre!
Ah, oile negre de rasă, care au urmat pe mii de ani migraţiile epice!
Noi am ros maximele înghiţite în gât şi stomac!

Pe acest tărâm, realitatea şi umbrele au devorat absurdul şi
Au devenit o viaţă de multiple carnavale în oglindă.
În fiecare noapte lumina focului
Îi luminează pe bătrâni şi pe copii,
Timiditatea fetei, surâsul cu gura acoperită, ochii visători,
Ah, aripile de pasăre gata de zbor între muzicuţa şi chitara lunii!
Acceptând o nouă viaţă, umbra flăcării aduce pentru prima dată
Uimirea pentru lumină în ochii bebeluşului.
Ah, pentru a întâmpina moartea,
Pentru a ajunge în sfârşit la sărbătoarea absurdului,
Ei sacrificau animalele şi nu era un joc,
Ci împlinirea despărţirii morţii de viaţă,
Niciun ceremonial nu poate fi pus deasupra, iar plânsul
Face ca şi alte animale să cadă odată cu piatra mortuară
Limbajul pietricelelor şi ciocanelor, care nu pot fi martori
La învierea din morţi,
Numai aici se poate, numai aici se
Poate simţi valoarea unui grup pentru o persoană.
Nu ştiu dacă e pedeapsă sau mântuire. Lumea de azi
Respiră pe coridoare smălţuite ca mercur.
Sânii mari nu sunt cu lapte, ci cu silicon,
Iar sarcina reproducerii revine eprubetelor albe.
Lasă-i pe cei dragi să se întoarcă, lovesc cu piciorul
Ca un bebeluş în leagănul corpului ceresc,
Nu numai pentru a alege limba maternă, de dragul de a vorbi,
Lanţul munţilor este craniul
La care spiritul nostru poate ajunge direct.
Ah, asta s-ar putea să nu fie epoca pe care noi ne-am imaginat-o,
Sunt din ce în ce mai puţini copii care pot

Recita genealogia eroilor,
Iar oamenii care pot să coordoneze cortegiul funerar
Au ajuns animale rare!
Cea mai mare turtă de hrişcă de pe pământ oferă puţin spaţiu
Celor flămânzi, slabi şi nevoiaşi,
Lasă limba veche, ca în noile legi,
Să devină carta acestei lumi!
Pantele organice în cuvinte, te laudă
Cu pietrele încinse, ai îndepărtat mizeria!
Să se bucure cei care forează pielea vacii!
Pinul care arde cu şuier uşor e întruparea tatei!
Munţii de pe ambele părţi ale coastelor,
Pantele abrupte ale pământului
Răsucite la stânga, munţii focului Heti Laba [1]:
Un banchet unde şeile negre se întâlnesc
Cu ornamente de-argint.
Descendenţi Nuosu [2], dacă nu aţi uitat
Ca de Ku Shi [3] să duceţi spiritelor ancestrale
Ulcele cu vin de salabo [4],
Mâinile închinătorilor vă vor deschide
Măruntaiele sării şi vinului!

---

[1] Heti Laba, legendarul Hercule al etniei Yi, el a fost cel care l-a împins la moarte pe Geje Abi, care fusese trimis de Regele Cerului să impună taxe şi a aprins o torţă pentru a nimici dăunătorii prin ardere. Pentru a comemora această zi, generaţiile ulterioare au iniţiat Festivalul Torţei.

[2] Nuosu, zona locuită de etnie Yi pe Muntele Liang, se numeşte Nuosu, ceea ce înseamnă naţiune neagră.

[3] Ku Shi, în limba Yi şi calendarul Yi are sensul de Anul Nou, cade în jurul datei de 20 decembrie a calendarului solar.

[4] Salabo, un vechi ulcior de vin al etniei Yi.

Cu fața la soarele etern, chemați și aruncați argint și aur fin!

Monedele celor două lumi,
La linia de despărțire dintre viață și moarte,
La umbra copulării alb-negru,
Au țipat, zăbovind îndelung
Doar pasărea cu ramura sfântă
Și-a păstrat paharul de argint pentru sine!
Nu este progres absolut și nici
Înapoiere în sensul modern!
Ah, ai dat destul de multă apă
Și a luat puțină sare.
Fără mustățile roșii de pe agata sufletului
La ce folosește o placă pozitivă?

Nenumărate scări de beton învelite în soare,
Aici, nu se aude behăitul caprei negre
Ah, acolo, departe, turma de oi sare de pe dâmb
Ochii cui îi acoperă praful stârnit?
Capra neagră este un sacrificiu
Indispensabil pentru venerarea strămoșilor.
A fost o epocă a inteligenței. Sufletul omului
E destinat să zăbovească
Prin văile nesfârșite ale vieții și ale morții.
Ei trebuie să se întoarcă în sălbăticie pentru a descoperi
Pâsla căsătoriei celor zece mii de lucruri.
Trebuie să se cățăre de jos până la locul cel mai înalt,
Să se zbată, să lupte, să călărească,

Să ştie jocurile acelea străvechi şi
Poate doar revenind la organele fizicului de aur,
Fiul omului poate ridica steagul masculinităţii şi al creaţiei.
Acesta este Tărâmul Făgăduinţei,
Ascuns într-o altă dimensiune a universului,
El nu există cu adevărat, corespunde frontierei abstracte
Neştiute, fără nume, a râului timpului.
Lanţuri de munţi, picioarele goale, armuri, hrişcă,
Pietre de măcinat, castron din piele aurie, chitara lunii, Mabu [1],
Cuţit de comori, pahar cu gheare de vultur, piatră comunală,
Nodul eroului, chihlimbarul, sutra sufletului, pâslă albă,
Vânt de munte, pedigree-ul familiei Yi [2], proverbe, epopei,
Amuletă, lege comună, ispăşire a păcatelor unui mort, flacără, armă,
Tată şi fiu împreună, băutură, vară, rudă de sânge,
Căsătorie, condor, înţelept, şa, haine,
Tradiţii, festivaluri cu torţe, războinici, locuri de incinerare,
Libera circulaţie, demnitate, moarte,
Cei care pot muri, cei care susţin negrul,
Cei inimoşi, cei pasionaţi,
Cei animişti, jurăminte,
Oasele şi sângele celor apropiaţi,
Identitate, recunoaştere, solemnitate, tipar, eroism.
Ei ştiu, de ce fiinţele umane trăiesc,
Ca fiecare să scape de coada pe care nimicul o adaugă cometelor.
Aceasta nu este o superstiţie ştiinţifică.
Divinaţia umană se află în mâinile sfinţilor
Profeţiile sfinţilor sunt adesea confirmate de oameni.

---

[1] Mabu, un vechi instrument de suflat al etniei Yi.

[2] Pedigree-ul familiei Yi, bărbaţii pot recita.

Acesta este Tărâmul făgăduinței,
Va trece ceva timp până când
Rasa umană va putea intra în stația sa de mare viteză,
Transparentă ca ziua.
Acei locuitori, viitorii descendenți ai acestei rase,
Nu au de ales și asta pentru că pot doar,
Din propria lor trezire,
Să câștige puterea consternarii, sălbăticiei și furiei.

Ah, Tărâm al Făgăduinței, atunci
Poetul lor poate fi încă-n viață, sunt absolut convins,
Deși el încă stă în picioare și cântă,
Torța aprinsă din mâna lui luminează lumea.
Dacă noi am văzut acel viitor,
În stația timpului, el arată ca doi frați gemeni,
Unul cu fața spre rai și celălalt către întuneric,
Și lumea devine mică în acel moment,
Apa de gheață arctică îți picură peste frunte,
Lumina lunii din
Deșertul Sahara e gravidă într-o valiză.
Și ziua aceea se-ntâmplă să fie
Timpul întâmpinării și despărțirii de spiritul strămoșesc.
Nu numai cei care în viață stau jos în jur și
Când duc la buze băutura din bolul de lemn,
Deodată zvâcnește fulgerul durerii și bucuriei,
Încoronează binele în natura umană, lasă răul
Să înceapă să moară de când se naște,
Și după ziua de azi binele devine singura virtute.

Lasă viitorului nişte lucruri jalnice, nu trebuie folosită sapa
Pentru a le face rău, specii diferite
Au supravieţuit milioane de ani în afara lumii rurale.
Durerea şi circumstanţele pe care le-au întâmpinat
Nu sunt de azi,
Numai că acest secol este mai lung ca înainte şi,
Din nefericire, primul lucru pe care animalele îl uită
E propria lor nefericire.
Fă timpul cu adevărat posibil în patru dimensiuni,
Lăsaţi seminţele bunătăţii să se întoarcă din nou
În uterul omului, lăsaţi cuvintele rostite de Russell
Către viitorii oameni să fie dovedite corecte
De stelele de pe cer şi de soarele patern, etern.
Lăsaţi diferitele limbi materne
Să capete o nouă viaţă în aritmetică,
Fiindcă sunt diferite moduri de gândire,
Mai degrabă decât pragmatismul raţionalităţii instrumentale.
Atunci când neamul oamenilor se va întoarce din nou
În pustie la lumina torţelor,
Chipul fiecăruia va fi acoperit cu vopsea în ulei de bronz,
Paşii de dans duoluohe [1] vor urma ritmul secret al pământului,
Pânza roşie de pe capul taurului va anunţa
Reunirea forţelor naturale şi a dorinţelor primitive ale omului
În stupul tremurător.
Înapoi la patul conjugal al pământului!
Fie ca fertilitatea omului să fie parte a greutăţii,
Acesta este festivalul vieţii şi, desigur, festivalul oamenilor.
Ah, Tărâm al Făgăduinţei,

[1] Duoluohe, un dans antic interpretat de femei de etnie Yi.

Râvnesc ca atunci omul

Să fie încă o parte a acestei lumi.

Constantin Lupeanu

（鲁博安译）

文学与丹

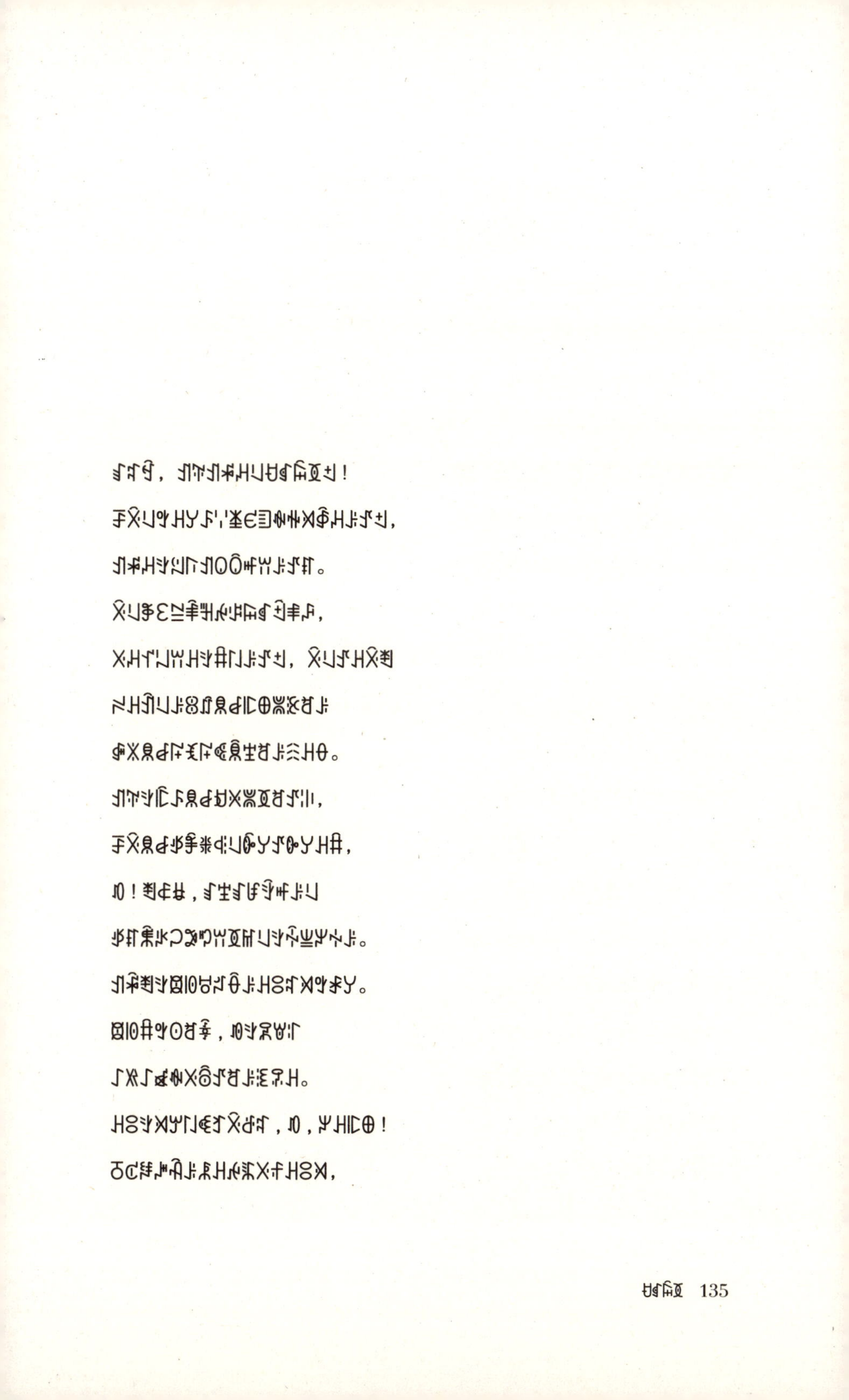

[illegible]，[illegible]！

[illegible]，

[illegible]。

[illegible]，

[illegible]，[illegible]

[illegible]

[illegible]。

[illegible]，

[illegible]，

[illegible]！[illegible]，[illegible]！[illegible]

[illegible]。

[illegible]。

[illegible]，[illegible]

[illegible]。

[illegible]，[illegible]，[illegible]！

[illegible]，

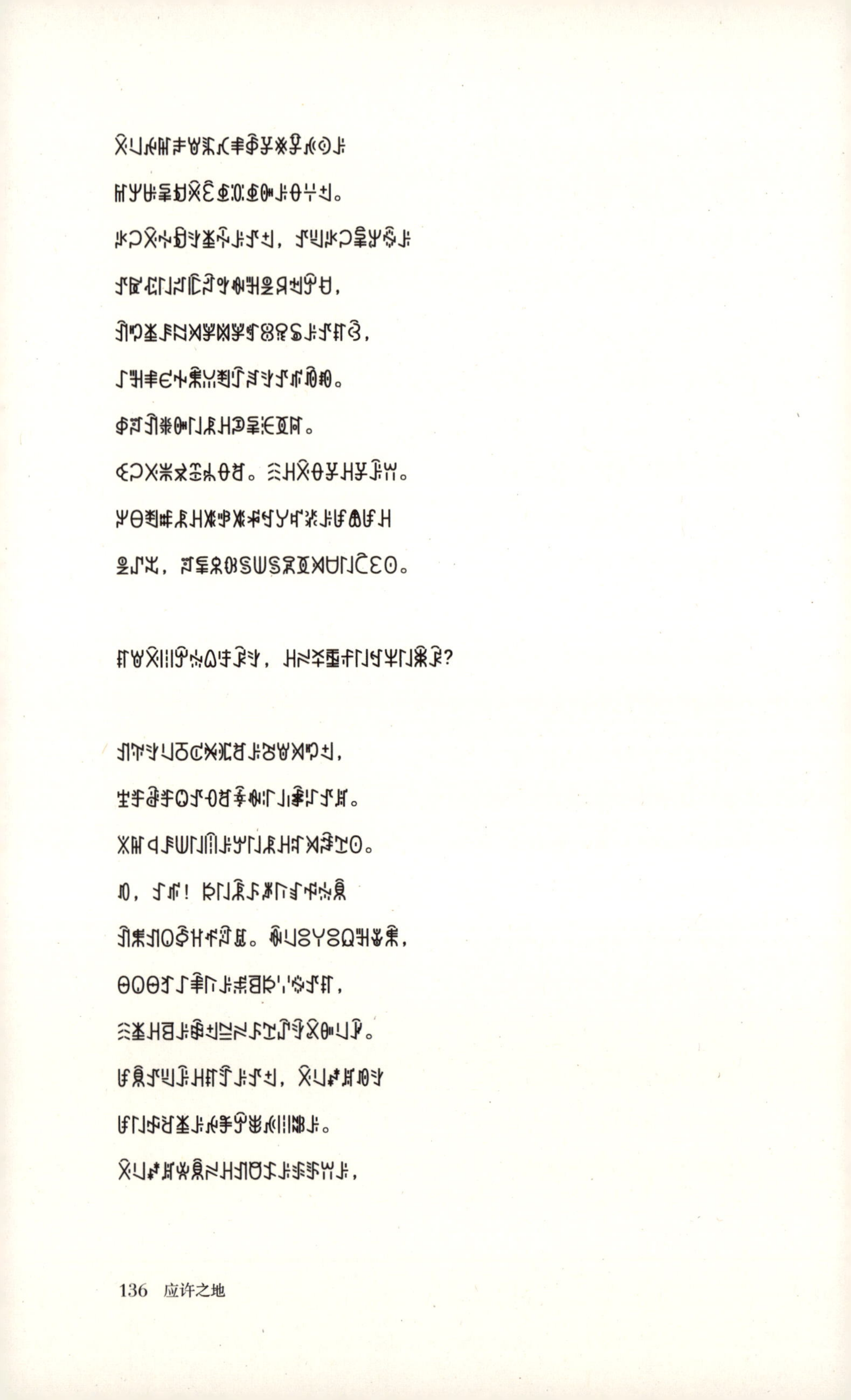

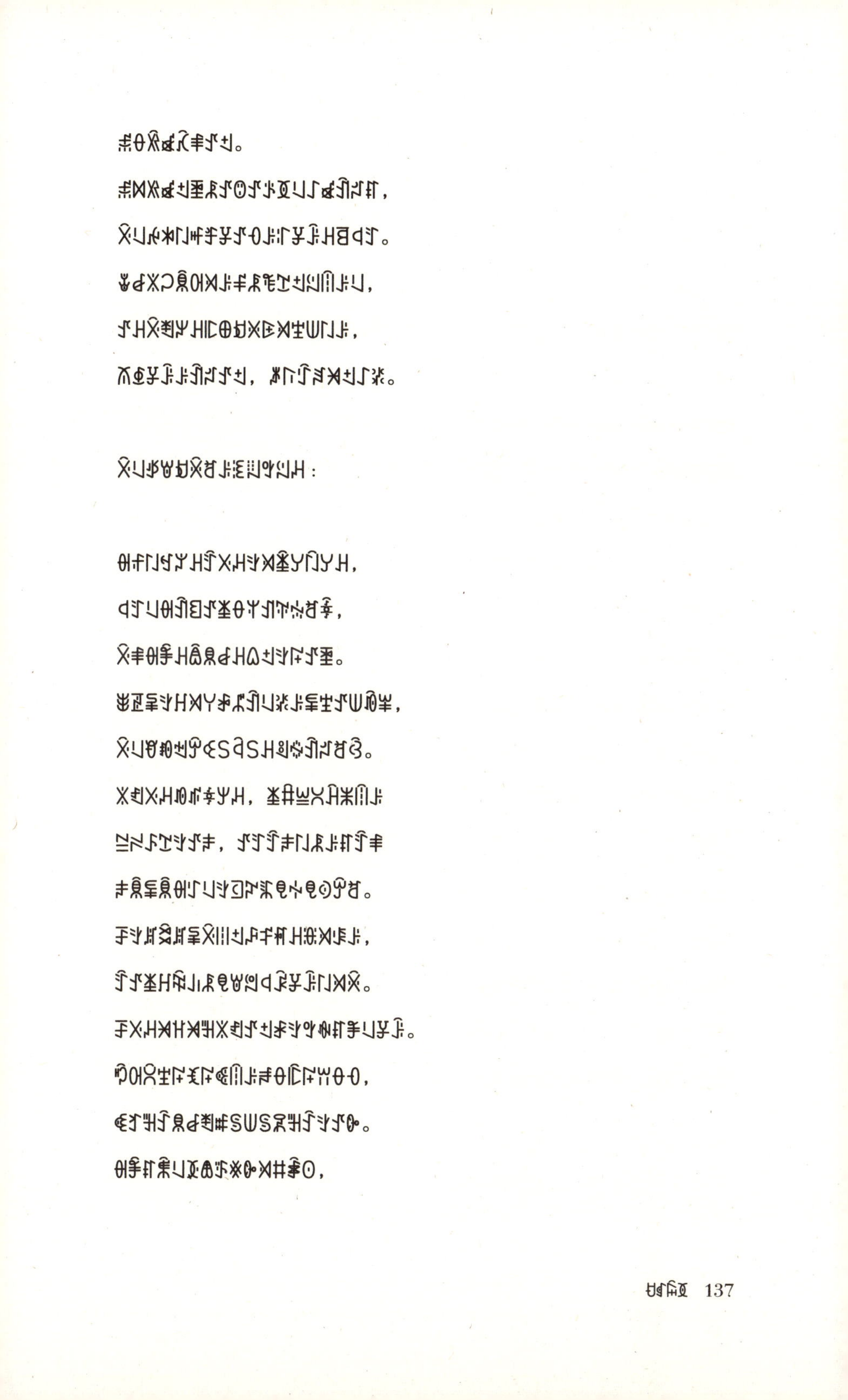

[illegible]。

[illegible]，

[illegible]。

[illegible]，

[illegible]，

[illegible]，[illegible]。

[illegible]：

[illegible]，

[illegible]，

[illegible]。

[illegible]，

[illegible]。

[illegible]，[illegible]

[illegible]，[illegible]

[illegible]。

[illegible]，

[illegible]。

[illegible]。

[illegible]，

[illegible]。

[illegible]，

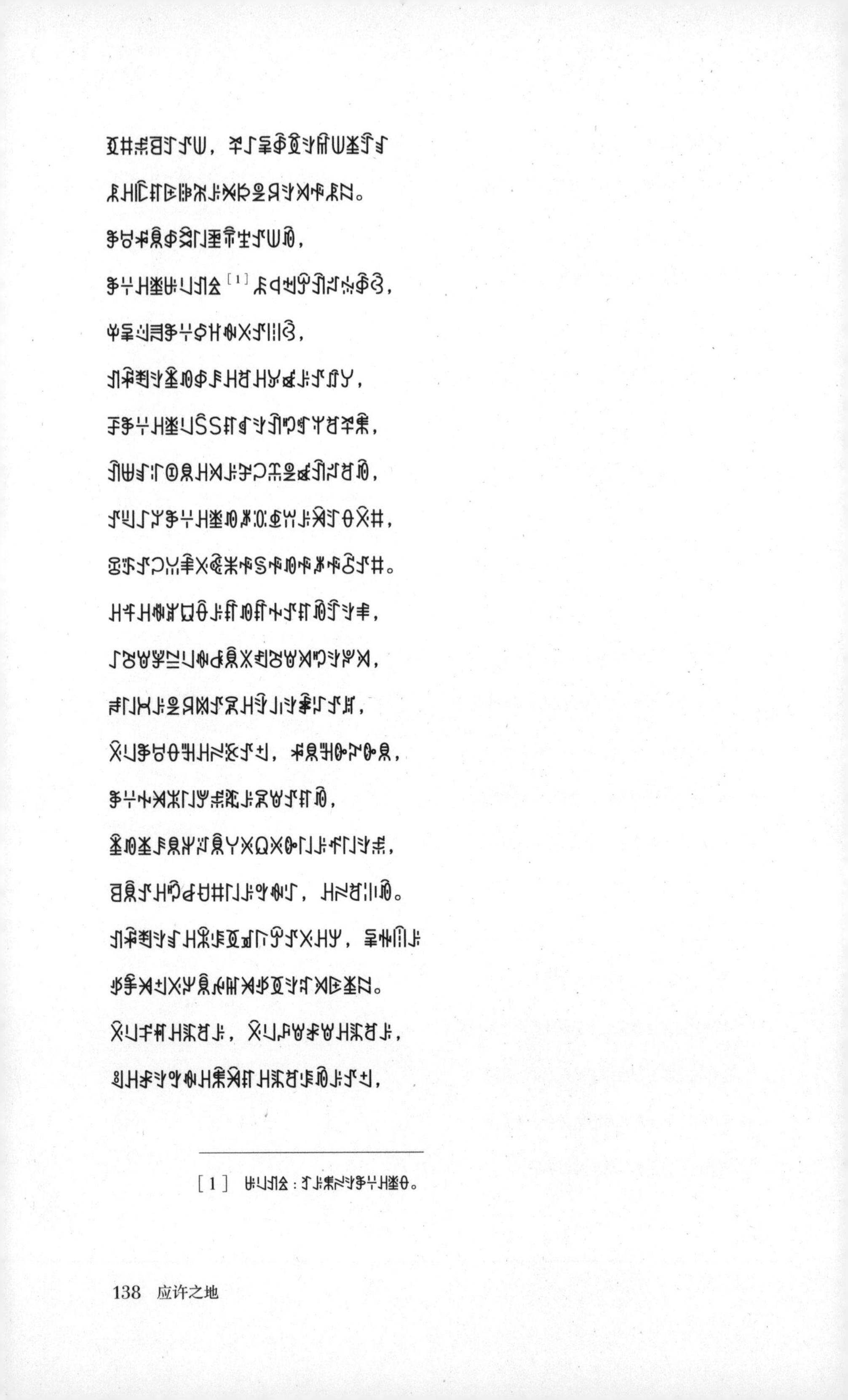

[illegible]，[illegible]

[illegible]。

[illegible]，

[illegible][1] [illegible]，

[illegible]，

[illegible]，

[illegible]，

[illegible]，

[illegible]，

[illegible]。

[illegible]，

[illegible]，

[illegible]，

[illegible]，[illegible]，

[illegible]，

[illegible]，

[illegible]，[illegible]。

[illegible]，[illegible]

[illegible]。

[illegible]，[illegible]，

[illegible]，

[1] [illegible]：[illegible]。

[illegible]。

[illegible]！[illegible]，[illegible]，

[illegible]，[illegible]

[illegible]，

[illegible]。

[illegible]，

[illegible]，[illegible]

[illegible]。

[illegible]，[illegible]

[illegible]。

[illegible]，

[illegible]。

[illegible]，[illegible]！[illegible]，

[illegible]，[illegible]，[illegible]，

[illegible]，[illegible]，

[illegible]，

[illegible]

[illegible]。

[illegible]，

[illegible]，

[illegible]。

[illegible]

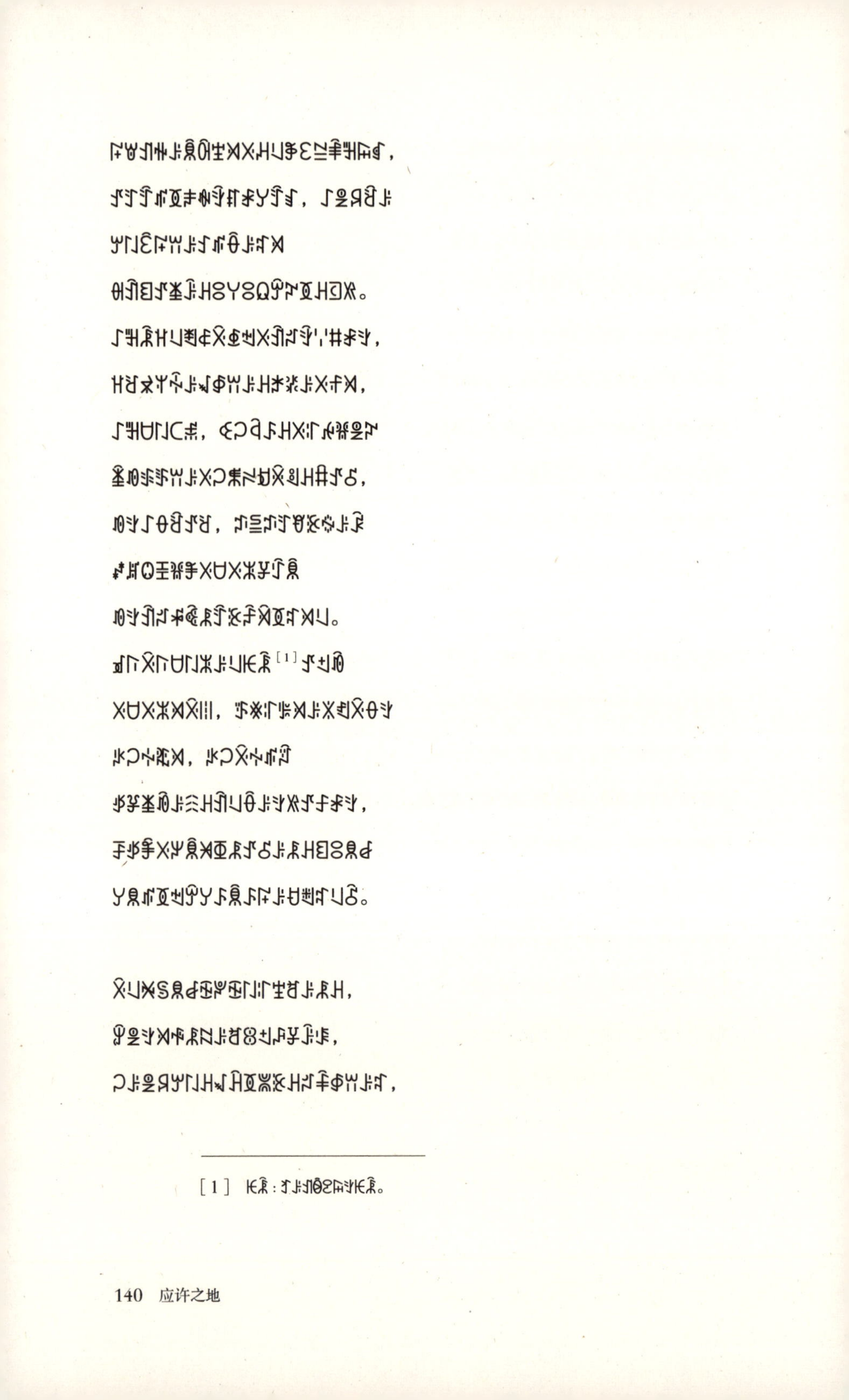

[illegible]，
[illegible]，[illegible]
[illegible]
[illegible]。
[illegible]，
[illegible]，
[illegible]，[illegible]
[illegible]，
[illegible]，[illegible]
[illegible]
[illegible]。
[illegible][1] [illegible]
[illegible]，[illegible]
[illegible]，[illegible]
[illegible]，
[illegible]
[illegible]。

[illegible]，
[illegible]，
[illegible]，

[1] [illegible]：[illegible]。

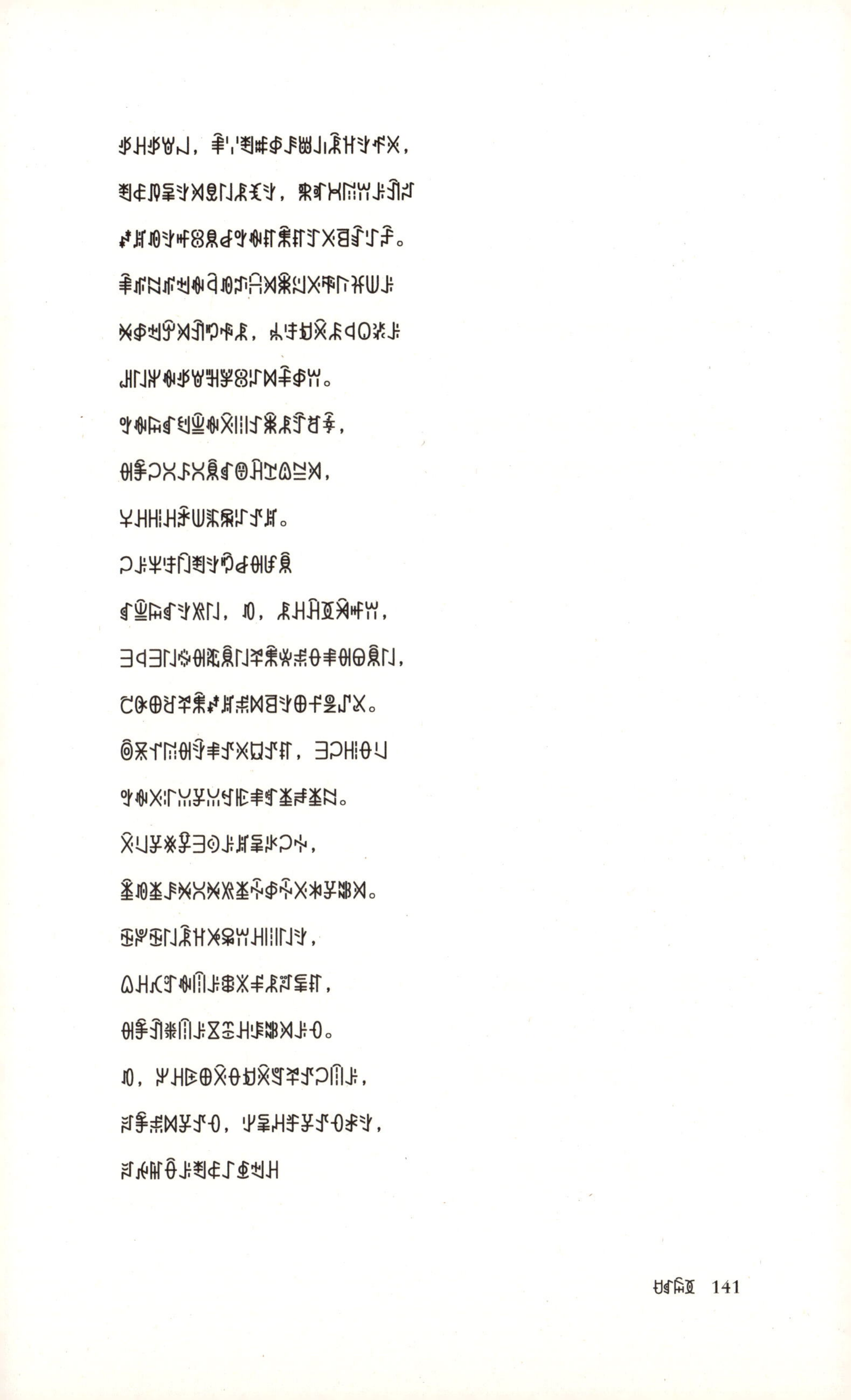

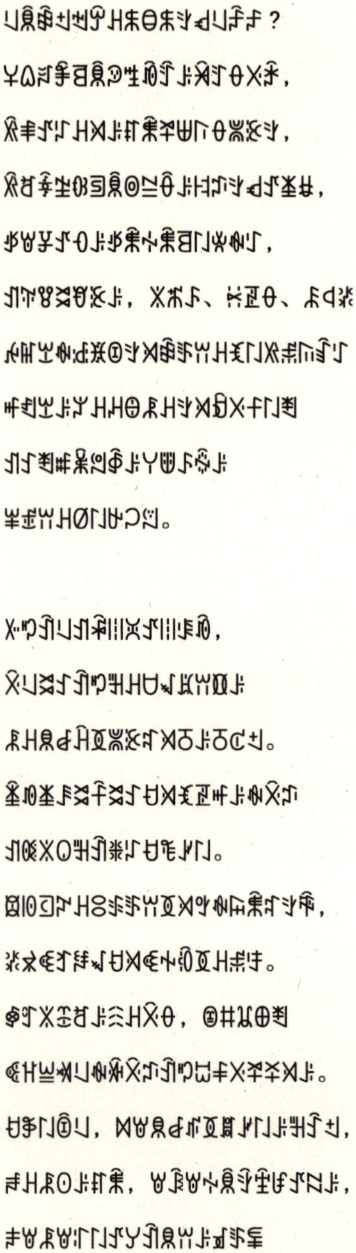

[illegible]

[illegible]。

[illegible]，[illegible][1][illegible]！[illegible]，

[illegible]

[illegible]。

[illegible]，[illegible]、[illegible]，

[illegible]！

[illegible]

[illegible]！

[illegible]！

[illegible]！

[illegible]，[illegible]！

[illegible]，[illegible]

[illegible]！

[illegible]，[illegible]！

[illegible]！

[illegible]

[illegible]。

[illegible]，

[illegible]、[illegible]、[illegible]，

[illegible]，[illegible]！

---

[1] [illegible]：[illegible]。

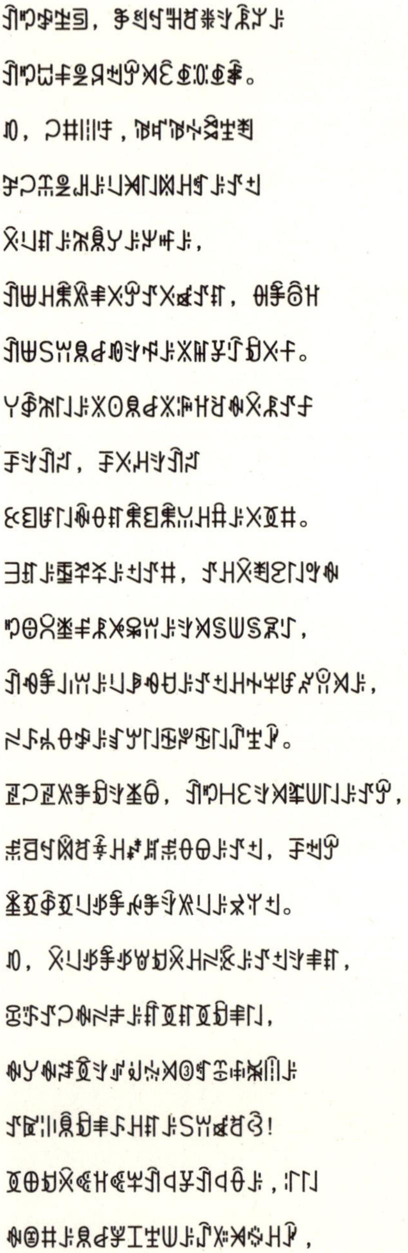

[illegible]

[illegible]！

[illegible]，[illegible]

[illegible]！

[illegible]！

[illegible]，[illegible]！

[illegible]，[illegible]，

[illegible][1][illegible]：[illegible]

[illegible]。

[illegible]，[illegible]

[illegible][2][illegible][3][illegible]

[illegible]！

[illegible]，[illegible]，

[illegible]！[illegible]，

[illegible]，[illegible]

[illegible]

[illegible]！

[illegible]，[illegible]

[illegible]！

---

[1] [illegible]：[illegible]，[illegible]，[illegible]，[illegible]。

[2] [illegible]：[illegible]，[illegible]“[illegible]”[illegible]。

[3] [illegible]：[illegible]。

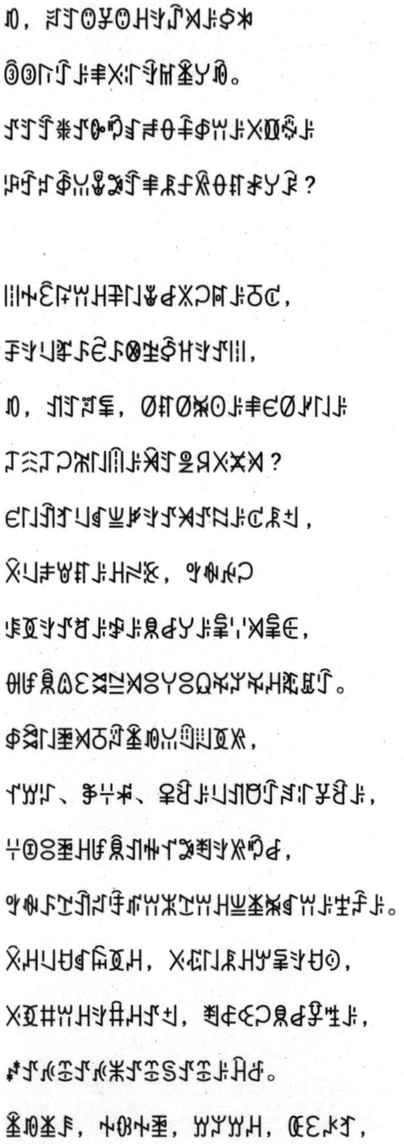

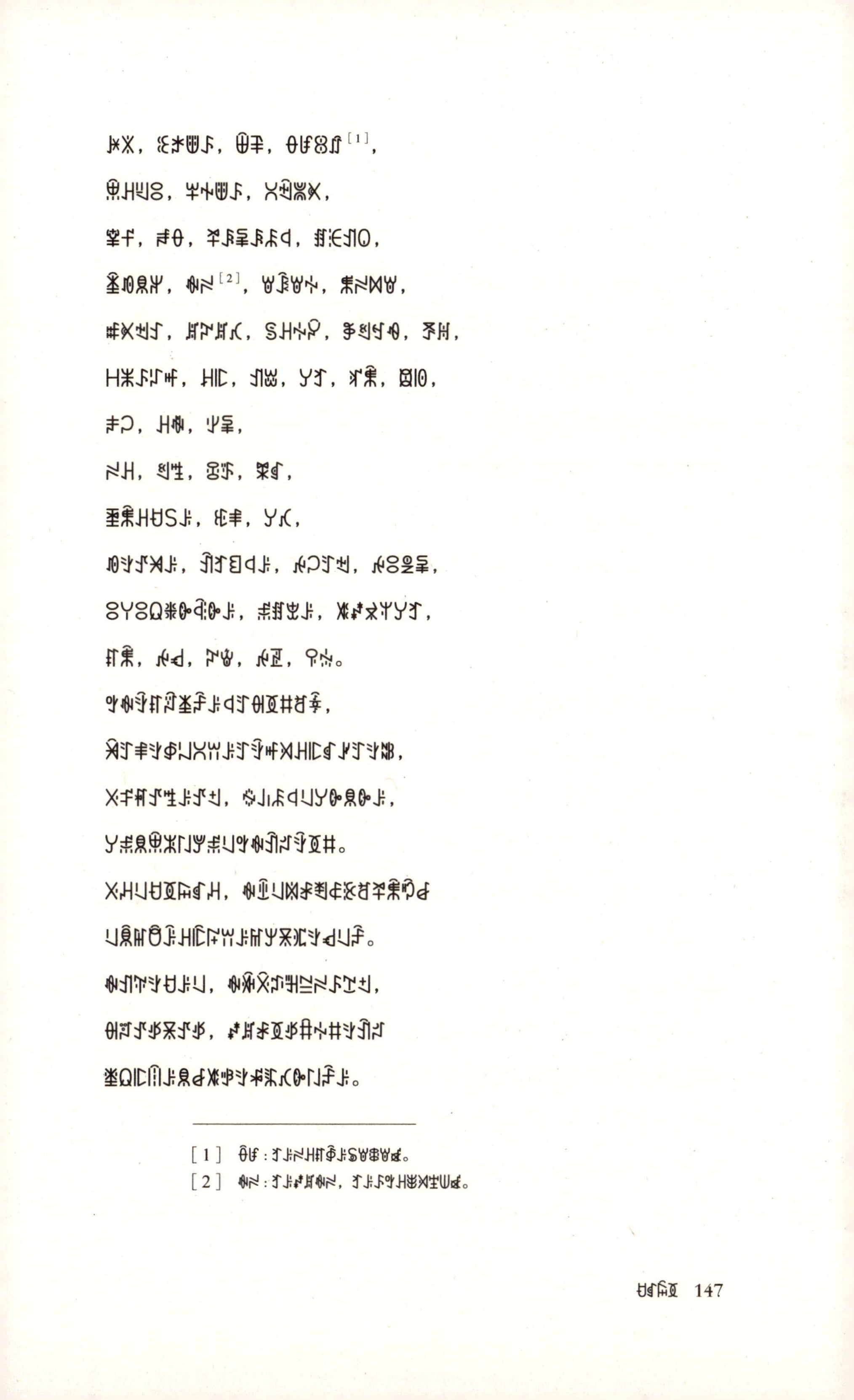

[illegible][1]，
[illegible]，
[illegible]，
[illegible][2]，[illegible]，
[illegible]，
[illegible]，
[illegible]，
[illegible]，
[illegible]，
[illegible]，
[illegible]，
[illegible]。
[illegible]，
[illegible]，
[illegible]，
[illegible]。
[illegible]
[illegible]。
[illegible]，
[illegible]
[illegible]。

[1] [illegible]。

[2] [illegible]。

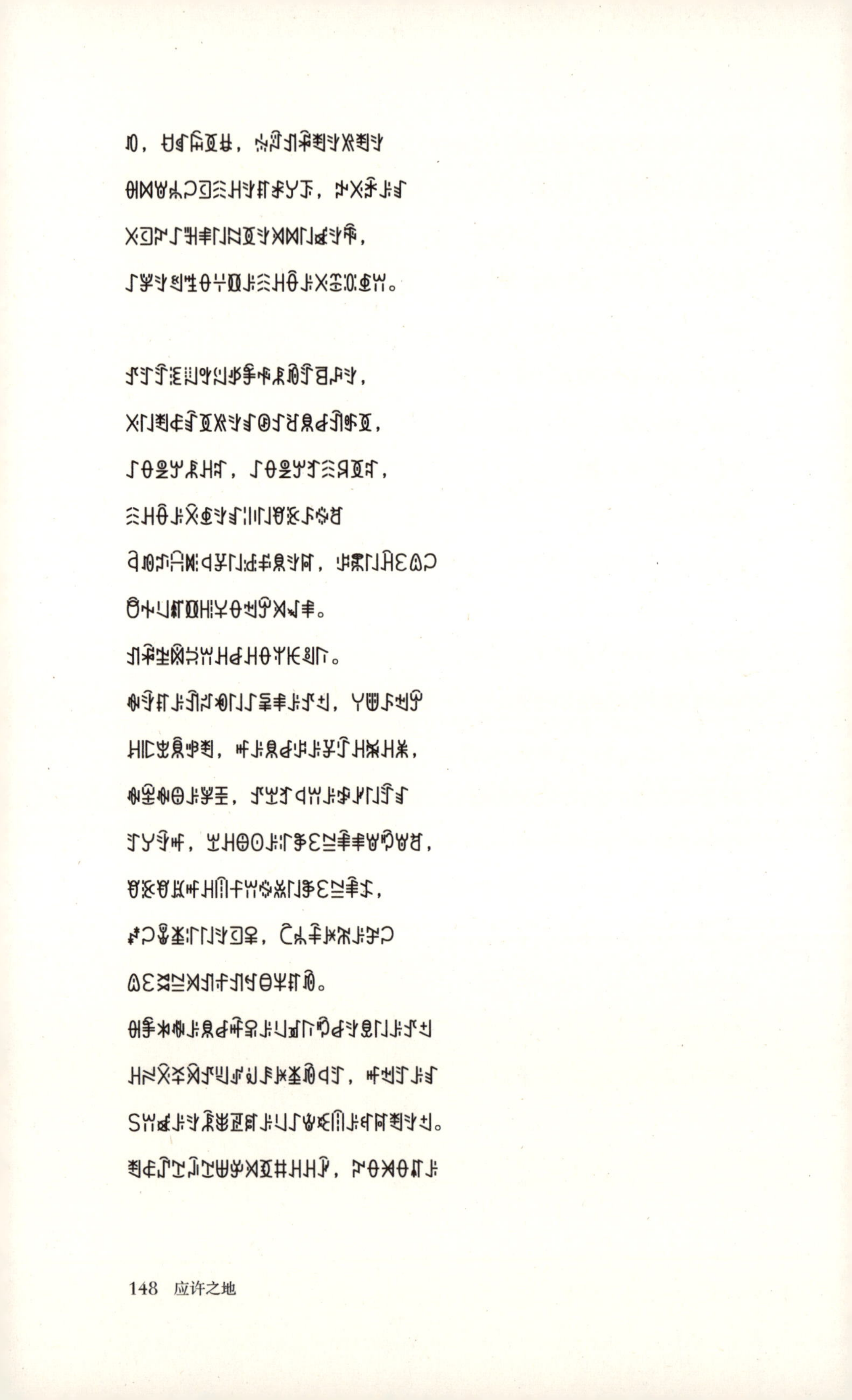

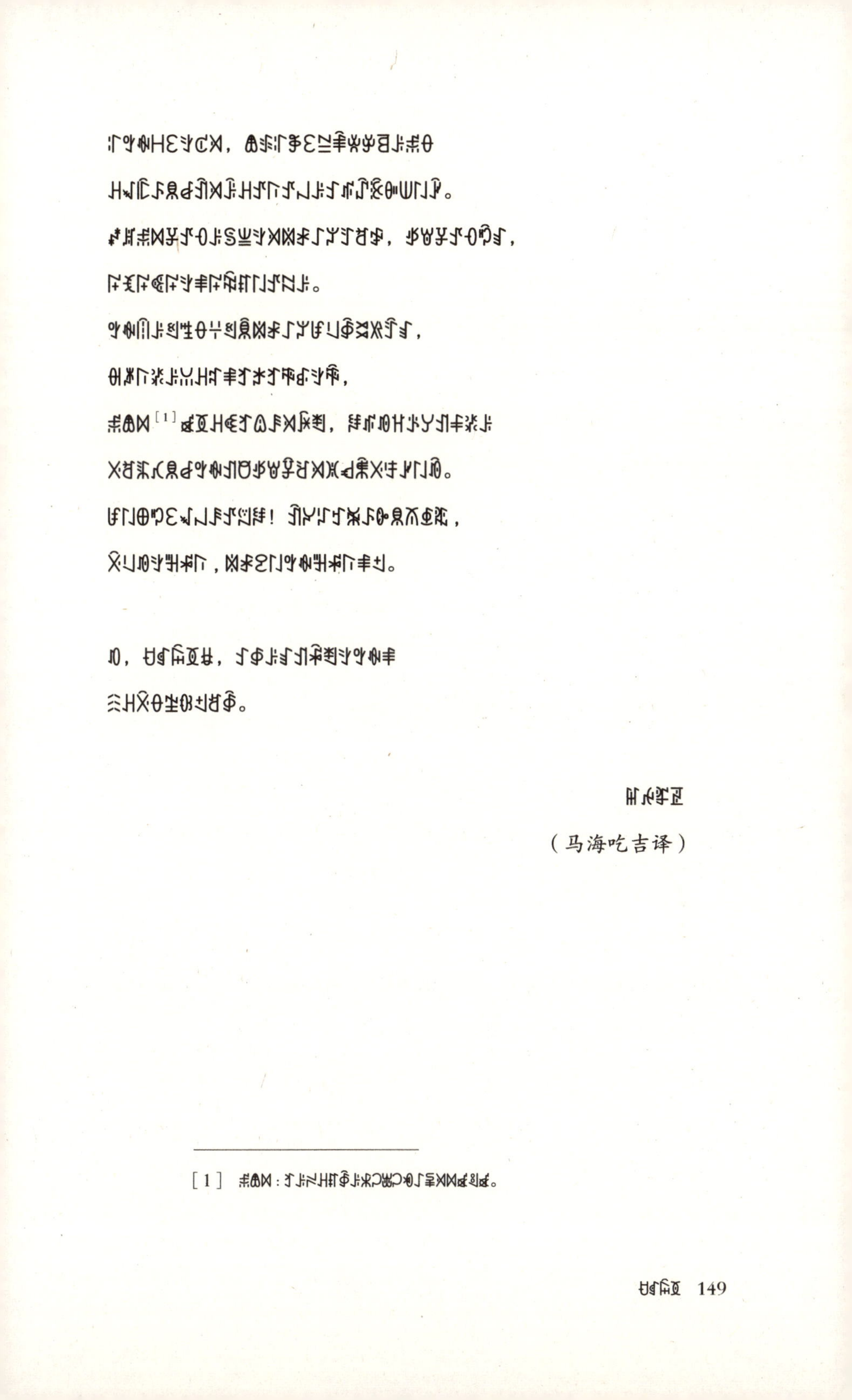

[illegible]

[illegible][1][illegible]

[illegible]

[illegible]

（马海吃吉译）

[1] [illegible]

代跋一

逆风而上的鹰与“历史的天使”

自近年来创作《裂开的星球》《迟到的挽歌——献给我的父亲吉狄·佐卓·伍合略且》之后，诗人吉狄马加又为我们奉献了一部新的长诗《应许之地》。初次看到这个诗题，我感到有点意外，待读完之后，我又感到“必然”——作为一个具有历史眼光、一直热切关注人类文明进程的诗人，吉狄马加写出这首长诗，乃是他长期思考和酝酿的一个逻辑结果。

诗的基本主题首先是对“现代性”的审视。早在一两百年前，甚至更早，人类从各个方面对“现代性”的追求已经开始了，时至今日，这种追求给我们带来了什么？我们是不是需要在这不断加速的历史进程中“慢下来”？换句话说，哲人们所说的“猫头鹰”是不是早就到了起飞的时候？而诗歌，是否也应担当起它的历史责任？

我想起了前些年陪美国著名诗人罗伯特·哈斯、布伦达·希尔曼夫妇游上海外滩的经历：望着对岸高耸入云的电视塔和颇为炫酷的后现代建筑，布伦达转过身来，微笑着对我们说："其实，比起那些高楼，我更爱你们西湖边上的垂柳。"

而我在当时颇受触动。是啊，我们究竟想要什么？人们为之骄傲的摩天高楼是否给他们真正带来了福祉？而一丝垂柳，在我们这里又唤起了什么？

这个"福祉"，也就是吉狄马加这首长诗所运用、审视、探究的"应许之地"。如长诗的一开始所说，"当然不是上帝许诺给犹太人的礼物"。它是历史给我们的一个承诺，一个现代或后现代乌托邦，一个更为光怪陆离的现代神话。

毫无疑问，诗人选择了这个重大主题，或者说，他面对这个具有全球普遍意义的问题进行创作，这是需要很大勇气的。这不仅是一种如今很多诗人都在回避的"宏大叙事"，这样做，也面临着巨大的艺术风险。如实说，作为多年的诗友，当马加请我为他这部长诗的出版作序时，我也感到很为难：这远远超出了我的能力。

也许，我自己更偏爱那种从个人的角度对生活进行审视的写作，如我前不久翻译的美国已故女诗人简·肯庸的一首诗《梨子》：

> 人到中年时会有一个时刻
> 当你愈来愈厌倦，被你自己的
> 平庸心智激怒，
> 害怕。

那一天的太阳
燃烧得又热又亮，
让你更加凄凉。

它发生得很微妙，就像一个
从里到外都坏了的梨子一样，
而你可能毫无知觉
直到事情已发展得如此之快。

从一只不起眼的、平时我们毫无知觉的坏了的梨子入手，却唤起了我们对自身存在的警觉。这样的诗，真具有一种让人暗自惊心的力量。

的确，我倾向于这类具有个人性质、在风格上也更为简约的诗。我也曾在文章中谈到 20 世纪 80 年代以来许多诗人的“史诗诉求”或对于“大诗”的雄心，但是后来呢？——即使是海子本人，对他的几部长诗恐怕也有一种失败之感。

但是话又说回来，那些对时代生活进行宏观把握的诗就完全“失效”了吗？未必。如果我们重读艾略特的《荒原》或聂鲁达的《马楚·比楚高峰》仍能受到深深的触动，我们就得承认那对我们的写作仍会是一种召唤。换一个角度来想，如果当年尚年轻的布罗茨基不认为“最主要的事情是构思的宏伟”（这是他对阿赫玛托娃说的话），会有他的惊人之作《献给约翰·邓恩的哀歌》出现吗？

这是我们所看到的诗人吉狄马加以及他在当今诗坛的独特意

义：他经受了现代主义的洗礼，他也深知诗歌艺术的限度和戒律，但他有勇气知其不可而为之。重要的是，他不仅要在今天恢复大诗写作的可能性，他也获得了一种与之相称的广阔视野，一种从容驾驭重大题材和复杂经验的能力。他的诗歌技艺也日趋娴熟。他可以与他所生活的时代进行一种诗的对话了。

这也就是我们看到的这首长诗。作为一个历史的承受者，诗人当然并不否定人们对“现代性”的追求，但他获得一种更高审视的视野。在这首长诗中，他穿行在“数字化的居住区域”、置身于“现代星球的漂浮物”之间，见证、评说，但同时又以他的信念和诗性想象力，打开了另外的存在维度。它唤起了我们的同感，但又促使人们去思索。纵然长诗中有些句子可能有些直露，但从整体上看，这部长诗获得了与它所书写的时代相称的恢宏、繁密和“复调”的性质。

面对全球化所带来的“世界的同一性”，以及到处所显现的“同一张脸”，诗人当然会发问：“为什么不让局部凹陷于整体的肚脐？”这样一个隐喻不仅新鲜独到，也很耐人寻味。诗人不仅要为世界的多样性和差异性辩护，从根本上看，他要为人的位置辩护，为生命本身辩护；在“穿越任何一个障碍物/都能在穹顶目睹到闪烁的电子眼”的时代，诗人看到的只是“科学的胜利”“技术的胜利”……作为一个曾经的“骑手”，他深切地意识到在当今“寻找马蹄铁的预言已经没有意义”。他索性深入到一个以人工智能来取代人本身的时代细部或隐秘处，体现了他作为一个诗人的异乎寻常的敏感：

吉狄马加画像　未未 绘

乳房的膨胀不是奶水而是糟糕的硅胶，
而繁衍生命的任务给了白色的试管。

如果没有了灵魂玛瑙上那红色的穗须
再积极的盘子又有何用？

“积极的盘子”堪称是一个词语的大胆创造。毫无疑问，诗人的世界观是“积极的”（最起码比我的“积极”），人们对现代乌托邦的追求和营造也要求我们“积极”，但这都不应是空洞的、虚妄的姿态。法国哲学家列维纳斯指出“语言的本质在于质疑”，诗人阿多尼斯认为诗歌的意义在于对现存秩序的“撄犯”。吉狄马加为阿多尼斯的好友，想必在某种层面上他也认同这种诗观。他这首长诗的重要价值之一就在于他对当今时代和未来富有揭示力的洞察，他对“现代神话”光环的去魅和质疑，他的不无痛感的警示：

孩子从电脑上收看偷猎者在北极
肢解海豚的过程，而书桌上的白纸
已被杀戮者意念的指纹倾泻染红。

如果没有这种来自语言的质疑，这种灵魂的考量和警示，“积极的盘子”最终会为我们端来什么？

这一切，也让我想起了海德格尔当年对日益扩张的现代技术和工业文明提出的深刻质疑。在一个无诗、无思，人被连根拔起的“技术统治”的时代，他也不能不思索人类的文明进程和所陷入的“形而上学的迷误”。正是这种迷误彻底破坏了人与世界的关系。正是在这个日益恶化的过程中，存在被遮蔽了，人从内里被掏空了，因而“技术的白昼是世界的黑夜”。

我想，也正是在这种背景下，这位哲人提出了“诗人的天职是还乡”的著名论题。

而这，也正好构成了吉狄马加这首长诗的对位性主题。“应许之地”这个诗题本身，就提示着一个诗人的“还乡”，一种对古老誓约的践行，虽然这一切又无比艰难，甚至不可能。

好在作为一个彝族诗人，吉狄马加有着其他诗人不具备的独特文化身份、语言资源和生命经验。在一个全球化的趋同时代，他转身返入彝族自身的传统，在他的创作中也有意识地对彝族文化资源进行发掘和整合。在《迟到的挽歌——献给我的父亲吉狄·佐卓·伍合略且》中，他别出心裁地写到彝族传说中一只以双舌著称的绵羊“双舌羊约格哈加”。显然，这体现了一种神话学意义上的自我辨认，一种要把自身中的文化多重性融为一个独特整体的努力。

重要的是，作为一个在大凉山和彝族文化摇篮中成长、“在梦里接受了双舌羊约格哈加的馈赠”的诗人，吉狄马加一直忠实于他的生命记忆和信仰。在一个现代工业文明和数字化的时代，他仍处在先人和古老神话的庇护中。不仅如此，在这首长诗中，他还要把人们重新带回到“久违的穿斗结构的天宇/以及神话中巨人的木勺”之下：

像他们的祖先一样向万物致敬。
他的声音在此刻是唯一的存在，
音质的骨骼支撑着光亮的天际，
因为他的召唤，河流会被感动
群山的肃穆超过了任何一个时刻，
每一个生命，就是那微小的昆虫
也会集合起自己的队伍，
赶去参加一个只为生命准备的仪式。

让至亲者回去，像婴儿一样踢动天体的摇篮，
不仅仅是为了倾诉才选择母语，这其中
群山的主体才是我们精神直达的颅骨。

诗人像彝族古老传统中的祭司“毕摩”一样招魂（而太阳“佩戴酋长的面具”），他的“还乡”也显然是“逆时代”的，朝向生命记忆的。他仍相信传统中的那种祈祷的力量：

当有人在耳边呢喃，反复地、持续地、善意地，
那幸运的斗篷就会从天而降
童年丢失的木碗将神奇地出现在眼前。

读着这样的诗篇，尤其是诗中“逆时代”的“还乡”及其诗

人形象，我不由得想起了德国思想家本雅明的“历史天使”。本雅明早年曾收藏有一幅超现实主义画家保罗·克利的《新天使》，即使后来流亡巴黎的时候，他仍随身带着这幅画作。他是这样描述这幅画作的：

> 保罗·克利的《新天使》画的是一个天使看上去正要由他入神注视的事物离去。他凝视着前方，他的嘴微张，他的翅膀张开了。人们就是这样描绘历史天使的。他的脸朝着过去。在我们认为是一连串事件的地方，他看到的是一场单一的灾难。这场灾难堆积着尸骸，将它们抛弃在他的面前。天使想停下来唤醒死者，把破碎的世界修补完整。可是从天堂吹来了一阵风暴，它猛烈地吹击着天使的翅膀，以至他再也无法把它们收拢。这风暴无可抗拒地把天使刮向他背对着的未来，而他面前的残垣断壁却越堆越高，直逼天际。这场风暴就是我们所称的进步。

如同这样的“历史天使”，吉狄马加这首长诗的抒情主人公的脸也“朝着过去”，朝向生命记忆中的家园，同时也任凭着历史的“进步风暴”无可抗拒地把他刮向“他背对着的未来”——那不可知的，不以人的意志为转移的未来。

不过也有很大的不同，在本雅明的“历史天使”的历史境遇间有一种巨大的、剧烈的张力，而吉狄马加的这首长诗更多了些东方的从容静观：“鹰仍然在宁静的虚空瞩望移动的印记”。这是长诗中很重要的一句。“鹰”一直在吉狄马加的诗中起落，所以他在这里用了“仍然”的字眼。它在这里再次出现，显然提升了全诗，并显现了诗中的某种动与静、上与下的多重对应结构。

正因为这种信念和超越性的从容静观，这种想象力的打开和毕摩式的招魂，在一个同质化、平面化的后现代世界，诗人为我们创造了一套动人的富有“磁性”的抒情语言，一个奇异的、万物相互映照和转化的诗性宇宙：

在山脉盆腔和腹部睡眠的磁性的族人
是太阳燧石的影子唤醒了他们。
鹰仍然在宁静的虚空瞩望移动的印记，
一只蚂蚁翻动土壤发出敏感的声音。

这就是生命的“应许之地”吗？是的，“它隐匿于宇宙的另一个纬度”。它超越了历史，也超越了任何地形学意义上的山川，如以下引诗中所说，它处在“时间铸造的玻璃那边”。这是一个富有想象力和语言才赋的诗人才能创造和打开的世界：

噢！应许之地，在时间铸造的玻璃那边，
不是夏日的雨季，在那无法确定的反面，
泪花与雨水结成了不可分离的轴线，
它让粗糙的山脉变得如同情侣的睡姿。

……而世界在那一刻变得很小
北极的冰水滴满了你的额头，撒哈拉沙漠
的月光在一只手提箱里怀孕。
而那一天正好是迎送祖灵的时间。
不是活着的人才围坐在那里，当木碗里的
酒送给嘴唇，同时滋长痛苦和快乐的闪电，
为人性中的善加冕吧……

多么动人！诗由对现代世界的审视开始，最后达成了这样的诗性超越和回归。“历史的天使”让位于或再次化身为诗的祭司。而诗人的职责仍是见证、创造和梦想。

因为这样的诗，我想起了马加一直所喜爱的聂鲁达：“因为他的诗歌具有自然力般的作用，复苏了一个大陆的命运和梦想。”

我不敢说诗人就达到了他的理想，但这样的诗篇赋予了我们另一种视野，另一种观看和思考人类世界的方式，同时，它让我们接过了久违的“木碗里的酒”，让我们麻木的嘴唇“同时滋长痛苦和快乐的闪电”……

我想这就够了，如果我们可以，如这首诗的最后所愿，愿我们都能穿过历史的风暴，为诗性的回归加冕，为人性中的善加冕。

王家新

As Postscript 1

The Eagle in the Headwind and the "Angel of History"

Following "Split-Open Planet" and "The Late Elegy", the poet Jidi Majia once again offers us an epic poem in the form of "The Promised Land". At first the topic struck me as an odd departure for the poet. But, when I concluded my reading, I was moved by a sense of inevitability. With "The Promised Land", Jidi Majia establishes himself firmly as both a cleareyed scholar of history and an ardent attendant to the course of human culture. There can be no question that these verses are the outpouring of a lifetime's rumination.

The essential concern of this poem is an examination of modernity. For hundreds of years, we humans have doggedly modernized ourselves. To what end? Can we slow the breakneck pace of history to date? Or are we, as some would say, already past the point of no return? If so, perhaps this poem undertakes to answer for our indefatigable "progress".

I think back to when I accompanied American poet Robert Hass and his wife the poet Brenda Hillman on a visit to Shanghai's Bund some years ago. Looking to the opposite bank, where loomed the Oriental Pearl Tower and other rather ostentatious specimens of postmodern architecture, Brenda turned to us and grinned. "I'd take the weeping willows of West Lake over these skyscrapers any day."

At the time, this moved me greatly. I instinctively agreed with her. What is it, I wondered, that we are actually trying to achieve? Have these skyscrapers improved our wellbeing? What can a lone weeping willow mean to us now?

What constitutes "wellbeing" is also at issue in the "promised land" that Jidi Majia holds under the microscope. The poem begins by telling us that this land is "not the gift the Lord promised to the Jews." Rather, it is a promise made to us by our own history. Our past and present weave a grotesque fairy tale of our future.

It requires great bravery to take on a topic so universal and sweeping in scope. Most poets of today go out of their way to avoid such colossal narratives. Tackling them puts one's own artistic integrity at risk. Frankly, when my longtime friend-in-letters Majia asked me to write the foreword for this poem, I felt the weight of the task. Merely reviewing the poem stretches my abilities.

I tend to prefer work that examines a topic from the personal perspective of one's lived experience, such as Jane Kenyon's "The Pear":

> There is a moment in middle age
> when you grow bored, angered
> by your middling mind, afraid.
>
> That day the sun
> burns hot and bright
> making you more desolate.
>
> It happens subtly, as when a pear
> spoils from the inside out,
> and you may not be aware
> until things have gone too far.

We can hold in our hand a mundane pear and, from the seemingly unremarkable event of its having spoiled before we know it, realize the alarming frailty of our own bodies. A poem like this stirs our innermost places and makes us shudder.

I'm partial to this simpler, more personal style. I've also written in past essays on the lofty ambitions and futile attempts of poets since the 1980s to create epic poetry. Even the few epic poems of Haizi himself were plagued by a sense of failure.

But can it be said that all poets who grapple head-on with our most universal questions do so in vain? Certainly not. When we consider how deeply T.S. Eliot's "The Wasteland" or Neruda's "The Heights of Machu Picchu" move us, we must admit that there is still a clarion call for such literature. Had a young Joseph Brodsky not believed that a magnificent rendering of plot and structure was paramount (as he expressed to Anna Akhmatova), would there exist today his stunning "Elegy for John Donne"?

This is the unique significance of Jidi Majia in the world of contemporary poetry: he has been baptized by modernism, he is profoundly aware of the limits and commandments of the poetic arts, yet he bravely persists in creating this kind of work. It isn't simply that he strives to restore the potential of epic poetry in this day and age; it's how he does it. The vastness of his worldview is commensurate to the task. He has an uncanny ability to harness and steer home the biggest topics and most complex experiences. He sharpens his skills on the wheel of time. His is in constant conversation with the entire course of his life.

We are audience to this dialogue in "The Promised Land". As an inheritor of history's mantle, the poet does not attempt to deny humanity's pursuit of modernity, but he takes a broader view of its implications. He moves through "this region of digitized dwellings" and stands among the "debris of the modern planet." He bears witness. He is a keen commentator. Yet, at the same time, he also wields his faith and his poetic imagination to tap into another dimension. He doesn't just arouse our empathy; he also induces us to think deeply about this world. While here and there certain lines of the poem might be a bit bare, on the whole "The Promised Land" reflects the vastness, denseness, and polyphony of the era it addresses.

Facing the phenomenon of globalization and, with it, the notions of "global identity" and the merging of humanity into a "single face," the poet asks: "Why not let the parts be sunken into the whole navel?" Such a metaphor isn't merely novel; it is highly thought-provoking. Jidi isn't just arguing for the diversity and disparities of this world; he is also defending the fundamental notion of people as individuals. The poet casts himself as a venerable horseman, riding through an age in which "no matter what obstacle one passes through / one can see the flickering electronic eyes on the dome." In the aftermath of victories of science and technology, he discovers that "the prophesy of finding the horseshoe is meaningless." He ventures into the nooks and crannies of an age in which human nature has been replaced by artificial intelligence. He responds with the unique sensitivity of a poet:

> Breasts swell not from milk, but from horrible silicon,
> and the role of reproducing life is given to white test tubes.
>
> Without the red tassels on the soul agate,
> what use are positive plates?

The phrase "positive plates" is a bold invention. Doubtless Jidi's view of the world is "positive" (at least more so than mine). Humanity's drive to build a modern utopia also requires "positivity," but this shouldn't be a vacuous or fabricated attitude. The French philosopher Emmanuel Levinas argued that the essence of language lies in the ability to question. The Syrian poet Adunis the imperative of poetry is to attack the existing order. As a friend of Adunis, Jidi Majia presumably relates to this view of poetry on some level. One core value of his poem is to expose the true nature of our present day and of the near future. Of the fairytale of modernism, shrouded in a halo of disenchantment and doubt, he offers this pained warning:

A child watches the process of poachers in the North Pole on the computer
dismembering a dolphin, and the white paper on the desk
has been dyed red by the fingerprints of the killers' minds pouring down.

Without this form of questioning, which stems innately from language, without this soul-searching and alertness, what can "positive plates" bring us in the end?

I think of Heidegger's The Question Concerning Technology. In an age bereft of poetry and philosophy, an age of "rule by technology," one cannot but ponder the meaning of human "progress" and the metaphysical delusions we've fallen into. These delusions have completely ruined the relationship between humans and the natural world. In the midst of this accelerating deterioration, some people vanish entirely, others are scooped out and live as mere shells of humanity. "The brightest day of technology is the darkest night of the world."

Under these conditions, as Heidegger argued, the poet's duty is to return home.

Herein lies the essence of Jidi Majia's latest work. "The Promised Land" is a journey home. It is the poet's attempt to keep his promise to the elders, no matter that such an oath may be impossible to fulfill.

As an Yi poet Jidi Majia benefits from sources of language and life experience that other poets do not. In an age of rampant globalization and cultural convergence, he delves into Yi traditions and integrates them into his work. In The Late Elegy he ingeniously reworks the Yi legend of Yoghaga, the two-tongued sheep, in a reflection of his personal identification with Yi mythology. Jidi Majia seeks to mobilize the myriad cultural forces within him in the service of his epic examination of the human condition.

As a poet who was rocked in the cradle of Yi culture in Liangshan, who "received the gift of the two-tongued sheep" in a dream, Jidi Majia has remained constantly faithful to his blood memory and convictions. Even in an age dominated by technology and numbers, he is sheltered by his ancestors and their legends. And he wants to bring the reader there, as well, writing, "he let us see the Chuandou [1] structure skies that have long disappeared / and the mythical wooden spoon belonging to the giant:"

> and pay tribute to all living things as his ancestors did.
> Now his voice is the only presence,
> the skeleton of timbre supports the luminous horizon.
> His summoning will move the rivers;
> the solemnity of mountains transcends any moment.
> Each life, even tiny insects,
> will assemble their ranks
> and rush to take part in a ceremony for life.
>
> Let loved ones return and kick the cradle of the celestial body like infants,
> not only choosing the mother tongue to pour out their mind; among these
> are the main part of the mountains, the skull our mind goes through.

[1] Chuandou is one of the two primary framing systems in traditional Chinese architecture. The Chuandou system uses pillars and transverse tie-beams.

Here the poet is like the traditional Yi bimo shamans ("oh Sun, donning the chief's mask"). His call to 'return home' is also a call to turn from the present and toward life's memories. He hews, still, to the power of ancient prayers:

> when someone whispers in your ear repeatedly, continuously, kindly,
> the lucky cloak will fall from the sky,
> the wooden bowl lost in childhood will magically appear.

Reading these verses and sensing their implicit imperative to "return home" and "rail against the times," I think of Walter Benjamin's "angel of history." In 1921 Benjamin purchased the painting Angelus Novus by his friend the expressionist painter Paul Klee. Even in exile, Benjamin carried this painting with him. This is how he described it:

> A Klee painting named *Angelus Novus* shows an angel looking as though he is about to move away from something he is fixedly contemplating. His eyes are staring, his mouth is open, his wings are spread. This is how one pictures the angel of history. His face is turned toward the past. Where we perceive a chain of events, he sees one single catastrophe which keeps piling wreckage upon wreckage and hurls it in front of his feet. The angel would like to stay, awaken the dead, and make whole what has been smashed. But a storm is blowing from Paradise; it has got caught in his wings with such violence that the angel can no longer close them. The storm irresistibly propels him into the future to which his back is turned, while the pile of debris before him grows skyward. This storm is what we call progress.

Like the "angel of history," the lyric protagonist in Jidi Majia's epic poem faces the past. He faces the homeland of life's memories, as all the while the tempest of progress whips inexorably at his back, turned on the future, an unknowable future that no human will can shape.

There is, of course, a major difference between the two notions of history. In the context of Benjamin's "angel," there is the mounting tension of extremely violent historical circumstance, whereas Jidi Majia's poem evinces a calmer, more Eastern attitude: "the eagle is still in the tranquil void looking for traces of movement." This is a crucial line. In Jidi Majia's poetry the eagle is always in motion, yet, here, the eagle is still. Here, the motionless eagle brings the structural implications of the poem to another level, introducing a counterpart relationship between the moving and the still, the high and the low.

Through a combination of deep convictions, of a transcendently calm view, of open imagination paired with bimo-like conjuring, in a homogenized, flattened, post-modern world the poet creates for us a moving and "magnetic" lyrical language, a strange poetic universe in which all things reflect and transform each other:

> It was shadow of the sun's flint that awoke
> the magnetic clansmen sleeping in the pelvis and abdomen of the
> mountains.
> The eagle is still in the tranquil void looking for traces of movement,
> the ant rummages the soil making a sensitive sound.

Is this the "promised land' of life? Indeed, it is 'hidden in another dimension of the universe." It transcends history. It exists in its own topography. It exists "where the glass is cast by time." This is a world that only a poet at the height of his talents and powers of imagination can access:

O, promised land where the glass is cast by time,
it is not the summer rainy season; on the indeterminable opposite side,
tears and rain have formed an inseparable central axis,
transforming rough mountain ranges into the sleeping positions of
 lovers,

...and the world becomes very small in that moment,
arctic ice water drips all over your forehead, Sahara
moonlight becomes pregnant in a suitcase.
And that day happens to be the time to welcome and send off ancestral
 spirits.
Those who aren't living are sitting around there; when the liquor
in the wood bowl is given to the lips, lightning
that simultaneously brings pain and pleasure,
crown the good in human nature, let evil begin to die
when it is born, let goodness be the only virtue from today onward

How moving! The poem begins with an examination of modern life, yet ultimately arrives at this transcendent message. The "angel of history" is transformed into a priest of poetry, with the imperative to witness, create, and dream.

I think again of Neruda, whom the Nobel Prize honored "for a poetry that with the action of an elemental force brings alive a continent's destiny and dreams."

I dare not claim Jidi Majia's poem as an ideal, but it is the kind of work that bestows a different vision, a different way of contemplating the human world. At the same time, he offers us a taste of long-lost "liquor from the wooden bowl," allowing our numb lips to touch "lightning that simultaneously brings pain and pleasure."

I've said enough. To the best of our abilities, let us all strive to rise to the poem's last wish that we might pass through the storm of history, crown the return of poetry, and celebrate the goodness of human nature.

Wang Jiaxin

Kong Yahua

（孔亚华译）

代跋二

吉狄马加的关键词

据古希伯来经典，以色列人的祖先亚伯拉罕，被许诺其后裔将拥有一片流淌着牛奶与蜜的地方，亦即迦南——以色列人出埃及后在旷野漂流四十年，终由约书亚带领而进入的土地。这就是应许之地（The Promised Land），是一个人与一群人命中注定的归属之地。对于吉狄马加来说，他的身份，也是他的自我定位，是一位中国的彝人之子。他与近千万彝族同胞所居住的大西南，从云南的哀牢山、无量山，到贵州的六盘水，直到四川的大凉山，就是属于他的应许之地——

在那个名字叫尼子马列的地方，
祖辈的声名是如此显赫，
无数的坐骑在半山悠闲地吃草，
成群的牛羊，如同天空的白云。

多少宾朋从远方慕名而来，

宰杀牲口才足以表达主人的盛情。

就是在大凉山腹地的深处，

这个家族的美名也被传播。

——《献给妈妈的二十首十四行诗·故土》

在这个炎天如火的盛暑，我有幸去到了大凉山的腹地，布拖，昭觉，受到过彝族兄弟杀牛宰羊的款待，俯就那反季节的火塘边微暗的火，听披着黑毡的男人用口弦和木叶说着灵巧的话，看姑娘们顶着灿烂的银饰和更加灿烂的笑容。这个尚黑的民族，凝重而横放，有着对太阳灼热的崇拜。这片土地的奶和蜜，是燕麦、苦荞与土豆，是壮如牛犊的野生黑羊，是丰富的光风水电。这是吉狄马加的血胤与方言所出的地方，一来到家乡，他那种自在和自由啊，从身到心都足可躺平，因为，“先人的骨灰仍沉睡在这里，/ 唯有无言的故土，还在接纳亡灵，/ 它是我们永生永世的长眠之地”。

所以，有时我们不禁会嫉妒吉狄马加。他不是一个人，他一写就是一个民族。这是一个跟汉族一样有着几千年悠久历史的民族，有自己古老的文字和历法，创造过十多部古代创世史诗。吉狄马加的诗，是这个民族在现代汉语中的形象代言，他是在用抒情诗的形式来写他的民族志，而这正是其使命与职责所在。在与阿多尼斯的对话中，他说过：“因为个体经验与集体经验在任何精神表达中都不会是没有关系的，我历来认为诗歌不仅仅是个人经验的一种表达，更重要的是它还要表现出与其他生命的关系，否则我们的诗歌就很难引起他人心灵的共鸣。”

这种民族志书写的精神取向，使吉狄马加的诗成为中国当代诗人写作谱系中独一无二的存在，也可以说，是一个异数。其风格的典型标志，就是他总是在共名的意义上使用他的词汇。在吉狄马加的诗中，河流不再是一条具体的河流，而是从彝族的创世史诗里流出；山，是神秘的力量的汇聚；鹰，是精神的图腾；至于雪豹，“我的命是一百匹马的命，是一千头牛的命 / 也是一万个人的命”，而不只是它自己的命。于是，出现在吉狄马加诗中的，“人”都具有“类”的意味，“民”都给人“族”的感觉。他的姐姐，是所有彝族人的姐姐；他的母亲，是所有彝族人的母亲。

所以，在嫉妒诗人的同时，我们有时也不免替他备感压力。一种资产的负累，使得吉狄马加罕有论诗即此诗的时刻，他的人物总是被置于深邃而广阔的背景之下，不是由其本义，而是由其引申义，而发挥作用。比如《最后的酒徒》：“在小小的酒桌上 / 你伸出狮子的爪子 / 写一首最温柔的情诗。”张力十足，有着清晰的即视感，但诗人立刻就给予虚化，提醒我们这是酋长的儿子，血液里布满冲突，草原的逝去使他一生哀哀嘶鸣。狮子的爪子是白描，血液里的冲突是评论，吉狄马加诗中的当下一刻经常不单独呈现为自足的意义，如果不同时隐含了一个人的一生，而这个一生又联系着众生的话。

这种共名式的写作，在最好的时候，确实能够创造出令人惊叹的杰作。如下面这首《致布拖少女》——

你细长的脖子
能赛过阿呷查莫鸟的
美丽颈项
你的眼睛是湖水倒映的星光
你的前额如同金子
浮悬着蜜蜂的记忆
你高高的银质领箍
是一块网织的悬岩
你神奇多姿的裙裾
在黄昏退潮的时候
为夜的来临尽情摆浪
你那光滑的肌肤
恰似初夏的风穿越撒满松针的幽谷
然后悄悄地掠过母羊的腹部

你的呼吸回旋如梦幻
万物在你的鼻息下
摇动一颗颗金色的晨露
你的笑声
起伏就像天上的云雀
可以断定
因为你的舞步
山脉的每一次碰撞

牛角的每一次冲动
都预示着秋天的成熟

精确而又如梦幻般的意象，大胆而贴切的比喻，长长短短的句子交织递进，构成曼妙的旋律。无论从什么角度来衡量，这都是一首美丽的诗。诗中的布拖少女是一个共名，在她的脸上，不可能有邻家女孩的雀斑，和昨晚与母亲小小怄气的痕迹。但诗人赋予了对象以不可替代的独特性，比如阿呷查莫鸟，就是大凉山一种长颈而漂亮的鸟。

我记得北塔在评论吉狄马加的诗时，曾经指出诗人偏爱使用全称的判断，比如“全部”“一切”“所有”“任何”等，以及具有如此内涵的词语如“世界”“宇宙”“人类”“永恒”等。这和共名式的词汇与意象一起，成就了他的崇高风格。在普遍躲避与消解崇高的当代，吉狄马加逆势而上地追求崇高，而且明诏大号地提倡崇高，正见其勇气与担当。而崇高风格所赖以形成的语言技巧，包括这样一种呼唤共名与全称的思路，吉狄马加显然对此有清晰的自觉意识：

伟大的高度，才会有
绝对的孤寂，迎着观念的
空无，语言被思想杀死。

——《鹰的诞生和死亡》

在与澳大利亚诗人马克·特雷尼克的对谈中，吉狄马加说："太阳啊，土地啊，河流啊，这样一些土著民族生活里赖以生存的元素，或者带着一些象征性的东西，其实对于我们来说都非常重要，已经成为我们集体无意识中的一个重要的组成部分。我们和土地的关系，和生活环境的关系，对土地的理解……""元素"和"象征"，他已经把握了自我风格之密钥。

吉狄马加的诗，形制上兼具匠心与魄力，近于声歌，宜于谱曲。我在大凉山，就曾在不同的场合听到过彝族男女倾情歌唱吉狄马加的诗所谱的歌，汉语之歌明朗而深沉，彝语之歌犷率而神秘。而我读他的诗集，则有一种感觉，觉得每一首都仿佛序曲，是为展开更为宏阔的戏剧性画面而预言的抒情性咏叹。现代主义诗歌的沉思与冥想，往往借助音乐的结构，造成内在的旋律，诉诸人的隐秘之内心。而吉狄马加更明亮的声音，编织着充满现代感性的语句，形成丰富的变奏，则有如高腔的谣曲，在无限广阔的空间反复回荡。比如美国诗人杰克·赫希曼所激赏的长诗《致马雅可夫斯基》，将救赎与重生的主题铺叙并不断深化，最终停驻于曙光照耀的群山之巅与人类道德法庭的最高处。那是连绵不断的乐句一波一波的起伏汹涌，但绝非泛滥无归，而是张弛有致，如赫希曼所称道的，"带着形象、韵律和呼吸的庄严"。

吉狄马加是具有世界性视野的诗人，他的诗歌胃口近乎饕餮，其营养不仅仅是他本民族的史诗与歌谣，也来自各国用不同的语言所写的诗歌。就我自觉有限的阅读面所及，他的写作风格更接近南美大陆的聂鲁达，加勒比海的沃尔科特，还有巴勒斯坦的达尔维什。他们的诗歌主题之一，正是各自的民族的应许之地。可是达尔维什的应许之地是以人质的身份来书写的，我曾经评论道：“巴勒斯坦人的自然是瘦骨嶙峋的，曾经流着奶与蜜的土地，剩给他们的只有巴掌大的干瘪一块，唯其如此，他们更懂得珍惜，更习惯凝视，凝视每一片云，每一朵花。而且，凝视橡树经脉里的水分，和紫荆树上细柔的纹路。”达尔维什、沃尔库特、阿多尼斯、吉狄马加，他们都是通过一种民族志的书写，最终写出了各自的人类志。

所以说，吉狄马加不仅仅是彝人之子，他同时也是中华之子，更是人类之子。他曾经说过：“我不仅关注彝族人，也关注这世界上所有地域的每个不同文化背景的人。作为一个诗人，如果没有足够广阔的视野和胸怀来关注这个世界，他也不能算是一个真正的诗人。”也就因此，应许之地对于吉狄马加，就从大凉山的腹地延展开去，扩散为整个中华大地，直到我们人类共同的家园。在《这个世界并非杞人忧天》一诗中，他早已开始了对现代性的批判。他看见今天的人类高举着机器与逻辑的镰刀高歌猛进，而无法摆脱这个地球遭遇不幸的生命在耳边留下的沉重叹息。现在，他又发表了新作《应许之地》，乃更为沮丧地发现，河流被切成数字的香肠，峡谷被寸磔为梯级电站，抽象的人将完全主导这个世界。他，呼唤自然力与人的原始欲念，让它们重逢于战栗的蜂巢。这是未来时代的天问，悲天悯人的诗人，乞灵于人类通灵的语词将赋予我们孳生不绝的力量。吉狄马加，“还站在固定的位列歌唱”——

他的声音在此刻是唯一的存在，
音质的骨骼支撑着光亮的天际，
因为他的召唤，河流会被感动
群山的肃穆超过了任何一个时刻……

江弱水

As Postscript 2

Key Words in Jidi Majia's Poetry

According to the Old Testament, God promised Abraham that his descendants would have a land of milk and honey, known as Canaan. We are told the Israelites wandered in the wilderness for forty years after their exodus from Egypt before Joshua led them to the Promised Land, a place to which an individual or the community was destined to belong. The poet Jidi Majia styles himself as the son of the Yi people of China. The great southwest, where he was born and raised, and grew up among nearly ten million Yi compatriots, extending from the Ailao and Wuliang Mountains in Yunnan province to Liupanshui in Guizhou and the Daliang Mountains in Sichuan, is the Canaan for which he pines and to which he dreams of returning.

All who lived in that place called Ninzy Manyie
Were impressed by the repute of our forebears.
Countless mounts grazed placidly on those slopes
Sheep and cattle clustered like clouds in the sky.

Streams of admirers came visiting from afar
To slaughter a beast for guests was proof of cordiality.
Deep in the heartland of Greater Liangshan
Your clan's good name was spoken of far and wide.

—24 Sonnets Dedicated to my Mother

In the sweltering summer of 2022, we bumped along the dusty track to Zhaojue and Butuo, two remote Yi counties in the heart of the Daliang Mountains in western Sichuan. Upon our arrival, we received the hospitality of the Yi folk and were treated to freshly butchered beef and mutton, roasted over a fireplace. By the light of the fire, I listened to the men in black felt garb playing the distinctive Yi music on mouth harps and bamboo fiddles and watched the radiant smiles of the girls, bedecked in splendid silver jewellery and ornaments.

Essentially animists, the Yi evolved a fervent worship of the Sun, the source of light and warmth, the fundamental element of life. Their equivalent of the biblical milk and honey is oats, Tartary buckwheat, and potatoes, wild black goats as stout as a bull, and abundant solar energy, wind power, and water. We have come to the very land whose blood flows in the veins of the Yi's true sons and daughters, and the love of music and songs remains the glory of these mountain inhabitants. Naturally, Jidi Majia, renowned as a major national poet and with an illustrious ancestry (he is a descendant of the chief of the Jidi clan), feels most at home when he is in his native land.

> The ashes of our ancestors still sleep here,
> But the silent land still receives the dead,
> And it is our eternal resting place.

This in itself explains why we Chinese poets and scholars alike feel a tinge of envy of Jidi Majia, the poet and the man: he speaks to and for a people. The story of the Yi is an ancient tale, as old as that of China itself, with its own script, calendar, and epic poems of creation myths. Jidi Majia's poetry is a proxy of his people in modern Chinese; he writes an ethnography of his people through lyric poetry. This is his responsibility and his mission.

In dialogue with the Syrian poet Adonis, he maintains: "I trust any spiritual expression of an individual is deeply implicated in the collective, and poetry—an expression of the human experience—must reveal our relationship with other life forms, the relation of the ideal to life. Otherwise, our work is paltry, insipid, and will not incite any ripples in the resonance of the mind."

This ethnographic orientation sets Jidi Majia apart from most of his contemporaries and peer poets, an anomaly, in a class of his own. A typical hallmark of his style is the use of generic pronouns. In his poems, each river has its source in a Yi epic, each mountain is a magical abode of mystic power, and the eagle is a communal totem, as is the snow leopard. "My life is the life of a hundred horses, the life of a thousand cows, the life of ten thousand men." So the poet declares, in utter solemnity. Thus, in his parlance, "human being" embodies the meaning of an assemblage, and an assemblage must necessarily belong to a clan, a tribal federation. Jidi Majia calls his sister the sibling of all who inhabit the vast remote domain of the Daliang Mountains; likewise, he declares his mother to be the mother of all Yi people.

While we marvel at the poet, we must also admit to a moment of doubt and worry for him. His characters, placed in a broad and deep context, in a crowd, at times give impressions of allegorical figures, abstractions, at most a type of human, pale of flesh and blood. For example, in "The Last Drunkard", we read:

> On the small drinking table,
> You stretch out your lion's paws,
> Penning the tenderest love poem.

The figure of speech is singularly fresh and bold, full of tension, and sharp in sensuality, but the poet immediately turns to allegorising, reminding us that he is the son of a chieftain, embittered and despairing of the shrinking grassland, and in whose veins flows blood thirsting for conflict. If the lion's paws are a sketch, the thirst for violence etched in the blood is but a flat exclamation. The present moment in his poems is never self-sufficient unless it simultaneously refers to life in superordinate terms, which must, in turn, be understood in the context of the whole population of a nation.

Such syntagmatic indulgences, at their best, can indeed give rise to extraordinary masterpieces, as illustrated in "To a Butuo Maiden":

It was in her bronze-like face
That I first discovered the colour of this land
That I first discovered the goose-yellow tears of the sun
That I first discovered the teeth marks left by monsoons
That I first discovered the eternal silence of the valley
It was in her riddling eyes
That I first heard the faint sound of highland thunder
That I first heard dusk lightly pushing the door
That I first heard the sweet sighs of the fire pit
That I first heard water-like kisses beneath the shawl
It was in front of her serene forehead
That I first saw the touch of a far-off storm
That I first saw flowers blooming from a stone
That I first saw the moonlight dreaming of lovers
That I first saw the pregnant April river
It was in the place where her beautiful image vanished
That I first felt sorrow and loneliness
But I'll never forget that day
On a Greater Liangshan morning pouring with rain

A child's first love was taken far away

Precise yet dreamlike imagery, bold and apt metaphors, and long and short lines interweave to form the quintessence of a lyric melody. By any measure, this is a wonderful poem. The Butuo maiden in the poem is generic. On her face are no signs of the freckles of the girl next door, or the traces of her bad mood with her mother the previous night. But the poet bestows some attributes unique to his heroine, redolent of the Abachamo, a beautiful, long-necked bird native to the Daliang Mountains.

I remember when the poet Bei Ta from Beijing commented on Jidi Majia's poetry, he concurred with the universal view of Jidi Majia's innate propensity towards universal judgment, generic pronouns, and words with such connotations as "world", "universe", "human" and "eternal". In all fairness, such cognitive penchant both mars and makes the artist, it appears.

Great height must sustain
Absolute solitude, against the idea of Absolute Void
Where the language is killed by thought.

—The Birth and Death of the Eagle

In conversation with the Australian poet and nature writer Mark Tredinnick, Jidi Majia asserts: "The sun, land, rivers, these elements of life are both vital for the survival of indigenous peoples and symbolic emblems, part of our collective unconscious, which also condition our relationship with the land, our living environment, our understanding of it." "Elements of life" and "symbolic emblems" are two keys to his style.

Jidi Majia has developed a remarkable range of themes, the best being wildly fresh in metaphor, melodious in euphony, and superbly crafted in structure. On various occasions during my stay in the Daliang Mountains,

I heard the Yi sing songs written by him. In Chinese, these lyrics have a transparency and smoothness to them, in contrast with their Yi version, chanted in much more raucous tones. Every time I pick up a book of his poems, I feel that they evince a cumulative effect to the extent that each poem serves as a prelude, an operatic aria, unfolding into a grander dramatic piece. Not surprisingly, modernist poetry often has recourse to structural music to create the inner melody and stir the hidden recesses of the human heart. Jidi Majia's luminous chants, with their rich variations of sensuousness, waft in the air like a penetrating ballad reverberating in infinite space. The long poem "For Vladimir Mayakovsky", critically acclaimed by the American poet Jack Hirschman, revolves around the central theme of redemption and rebirth, deepening in intensity before ascending to the summit and the highest court of human morality, illuminated by eternal sunshine. His lines cascade forth, as huge breakers crashing upon a rocky shoreline. The effect varies between convincing utterance and genuine eloquence, without affectation, strong proof of the formality of a settled style, as Hirschman comments: "majestic in form, rhyme, and breath".

Jidi Majia has a global vision whose poetry has a voracious appetite, nourished by his people's historical verses and songs, and by poems from all corners of the world. To the best of my understanding, his writing style is close to that of Neruda in South America, Walcott in the Caribbean, and Darwish in Palestine. Remarkably, all these poets share an inveterate longing for a utopia, figuratively and literally in terms of the theme of the Promised Land. On Darwish, as a hostage of history, I once commented:

Nature in the land called Palestine must necessarily be emaciated, grey, bone dry, as the Palestinians are reserved so mean a tract of land, the size of a palm, of the massive landmass, the once blessed Canaan, their dear homestead in memory, that once flowed with milk and honey; on account of this territorial scarcity, they know how to cherish what they have. They have learned to lovingly savour a single gaze at the billowing of the clouds in the sky and the gentle swaying of each blade of grass or nameless flower in the breeze. They feel the delightful moisture in the meridians of an oak tree and the velvet texture of a redbud tree.

One detects that a moment of significant choice occurs for Darwish, Walcott, Adonis, and Jidi Majia, all of whom have written ethnographies of their people, by which they have ultimately composed a story of humankind.

Therefore, I would reiterate Jidi Majia is not only the son of the Yi people but also of the Chinese people, of all humanity. He once testified: "My concerns are with my own Yi compatriots, and with all folk on earth, regardless of religion, region, race, language. A poet who automatically renounces his responsibilities for this troubled world and refuses to engage looks to be a sham, a pitiable conceit." The same must be said of the Promised Land envisioned by Jidi Majia to extend from the great Daliang Mountain region of his ancestral hearth to the whole of China, the entire planet. In a poem titled "The Fears We Entertain Are Not Imaginary", he fires the first salvo of attacks on modernity (on the instrumental plane). He bemoans humanity's inexorable march of industrialisation, a pair of sickles in hand and the cold logic of Instrumental Reason in mind—two deadly enemies of justice and happiness. He laments the plight of wretched souls languishing en masse, in every corner of this global village.

Now, with the publication of The Promised Land, a nightmarish exploration and scathing critique of the new waves of the modernisation drive that wreak havoc on his beloved homeland—rivers sliced into pieces like sausages and canyons dismembered into stepped power stations, with artificial intelligence dominating the world. Like a prophet in the wilderness, he steps up to summon all natural forces and primal human desires, gathering them in “the trembling hive”. It is a prophetic question for the higher powers posed by a poet sympathetic to the present human condition; through words with the poignancy of a spirit medium, we are bestowed with regenerative power. Behold! Jidi Majia, the poet and the man, “still, standing on the fixed pedestal, singing loud, singing strong”.

His voice was all that existed at that moment,
The bones of sound support the bright sky,
Because of his call, the river will be moved
The mountains are more solemn than any moment...

Jiang Ruoshui

Louis Zen（译）